A FAMILY OF HER OWN

SECOND CHANCE REGENCY ROMANCE (BOOK 3)

ROSE PEARSON

A FAMILY OF HER OWN

PROLOGUE

Watton House, Alnerton, 1818

The yuletide season was half done, as family and friends gathered at Watton House for the Watts' traditional Christmas Eve party. Everyone in the house was in merry spirits, glad to be reunited and happy that they had so much to be grateful for. Sophie Lefebvre had joined her dear friend, Lady Charlotte Watts, and the inimitable Mrs. Watts this afternoon, in decorating the entire house with evergreens. Garlands of holly and ivy were strewn artfully over every available surface, and kissing balls of rosemary and mistletoe hung in hallways and doorways, so those who wished might steal a kiss from a loved one. A mountain of gifts that would not be opened until Twelfth Night stood in the corner of the parlor, near the fire – which crackled in the hearth, loud enough to punctuate your sentences.

William Pierce, Earl Cott, and his friend Claveston St. John, the Earl of Wycliff, stood with Mr. Watts and the Duke of Mormont by the mantel discussing matters of business, as they so often did. Mrs. Watts sat with Charlotte and her new baby, Emily, on a red velvet chaise, recently purchased on a rare trip to London. Lady Charlotte's husband, Captain James Watts, and Lord William's new wife, Lady Mary, played on the floor with Charlotte's son from a previous marriage, George.

Cook had outdone herself, as she always did at Christmas. She had laid on a fine spread of cold roasted meats, soups and cheeses, mince pies, tansy pudding, and Charlotte Russe, accompanied by a rum-spiked posset and a richly spiced mulled wine.

"I am glad you were able to come, Father," Charlotte said, smiling up at the Duke of Mormont as she caressed the soft, downy head of her infant daughter.

"Yes, we feared you would not find the time to visit with us this year," Mrs. Watts added.

Though she could only claim to be the step-grand-mother of darling Emily, and even less to little George as he was the child of Lady Charlotte's first marriage, Mrs. Watts was a very doting admirer of both children. Sophie couldn't blame her, as Emily was as precious a babe as she'd ever seen and George a lively, but delightful boy. He had taken to being a big brother with good grace, and paid attention to his sister's every need, rushing in from whatever he might be up to if she cried, and holding her carefully whenever permitted. It was quite the pleasure to see such tenderness and affection in one so young.

"Yes," Lord William said, smiling at his father. "I am

glad your business in the North allowed you to return in time to be with family and friends this Yuletide."

The duke bowed graciously, but his gentle blush told Sophie that he was touched that his presence seemed so welcome. He was known for his prickly character and rarely had time for the pleasures of life – preferring to spend most of his considerable energies upon the running of his estates and the management of his investments. "How could I possibly refuse, when there is so much to be grateful for this Christmas, and such a fine repast to be enjoyed." He gestured towards the bountiful table, almost groaning under the weight of the dishes set upon it.

Everyone smiled. "Cook has prepared a fine feast, that is certain," Captain Watts commented, helping himself to a mince pie as he moved to kiss his wife upon her cheek. Charlotte blushed at the act, but the smile on her face showed the great affection between them.

"She certainly has," his father, Mr. Watts, agreed. "Now, who would like to join me in a hand of whist?" He indicated the card table set up in the corner of the room. William and Lord Wycliffe sat down around it after filling their glasses with more of the mulled wine and waited for Mr. Watts and the duke to take their places. Soon, their game, though good-natured enough, grew more competitive and their cries and moans made the women laugh.

Sophie watched from her seat by the window, her eyes drifting from one small group to the other. Everyone had their place and knew where they belonged in this warm and welcoming family. William, Captain Watts, and Lord Wycliffe had known one another since they were young and had attended school and university together. Charlotte was the sister of William, the wife of Captain Watts, and mother to the two children. Mrs. Watts had been William and Charlotte's nurse and had married Mr. Watts who was not only the duke's solicitor but his friend. Their bonds were long-standing and unbreakable.

Yet Sophie knew that her place here was tenuous at best. She knew that Charlotte looked upon her as a friend - and Sophie valued the young woman's affections and returned them most gratefully - but such sentiment did not change the fact that she had come into Charlotte's service as a paid companion. Despite the welcoming nature of the company here tonight and her years in Charlotte's service, in recent months she'd come to feel isolated from them all.

She wasn't sure when it happened, precisely, but if she had to hazard a guess, it was soon after Charlotte and Captain Watts had married. During Charlotte's first marriage, to the Earl of Benton, she had valued Sophie's presence as he had been often away. Upon his passing, Charlotte had needed Sophie as a shoulder to cry on, then as a friend in her struggle to win the man she had loved since she was a girl.

But Charlotte had finally won her dashing captain, and the evidence of their happiness was plain to see. Charlotte's attentions were now solely focused upon her husband and the new family they'd created – as it should be, and little Emily's birth had only further cemented their affections for one another. Yet, it meant that Sophie's position was tenuous at best, and obsolete at worst. Charlotte now needed a nanny, no longer a lady's companion. Sophie would soon have to think upon her future because it seemed unlikely that she would be able to remain here indefinitely – though she might wish to.

"Do pass her here, Charlotte," Mrs. Watts said reaching for baby Emily. "Why don't you accompany George on the pianoforte? I know he's been learning some carols especially for tonight?"

George beamed, and Charlotte reluctantly passed her child to Mrs. Watts. "I think that a wonderful idea, don't you, George?"

"Yes, Mama," George said, hurrying to fetch his book of carols from the music rack beside the pianoforte. He handed the music to his mother who helped him up onto the broad stool and sat down beside him. She flexed her long fingers then placed them upon the keys, playing a couple of swift arpeggios to warm them up, before launching into an enthusiastic, if not perfect, rendition of O Come All Ye Faithful, followed by The Twelve Days of Christmas. George sang proudly, his little chest puffed out, delighted to have all eyes upon him.

Sophie smiled on the outside and clapped for each song with the delight they deserved, but inside she felt sad. She did not begrudge any member of this wonderful family their happiness, but it sometimes hurt that such pleasures would never be hers. At twenty-eight, she was well past the age where she might secure a husband and have children of her own, and whilst she'd not felt the lack before now, since Emily's arrival Sophie had found herself wishing that she might become a wife and mother, too.

The carols over, Charlotte took her place at the card table, displacing Lord Wycliffe, who prepared himself a plate of food and moved to sit by Sophie on the window seat. He looked around the room admiringly. "You truly have everything you need, Lady Watts," he said between bites of a particularly good Stilton. "Your husband and children, and your former nurse," he nodded towards Mrs. Watts, "and might I say, that in Mrs. Watts you are also blessed to have a good friend at your side. Such fortune is yours."

Charlotte smiled and Mrs. Watts blushed as she nodded her agreement that she was indeed more than just Lady Charlotte's old nurse and her husband's step-mother. "Thank you, Lord Wycliffe. I do indeed feel blessed to have the very best of people around me."

"You have so many doting assistants now that poor Miss Lefebvre has hardly anything to do," he chuckled. Sophie prickled. How could he have so read her mind? She had only met the Earl of Wycliffe once before, at Lord William and Lady Mary's wedding, earlier in the year. He had asked her to dance, which had been most gallant of him, and she had been very grateful.

"First you do not include her in your list, and now it appears that you are suggesting that dear Sophie is not needed," Charlotte said, raising an eyebrow quizzically. "I do hope that I am mistaken in your meaning, my Lord, for I can assure you that she is still my most treasured companion. I should be lost without her."

Lord Wycliffe didn't look at all chastened by Charlotte's gentle scolding. "She would be better put to use at Compton," he said with a shrug. "My sister, Gertrude, is in dire need of a governess, someone who can guide her into Society, teach her comportment and manners." He glanced at Sophie his eyes full of mischief. "And it wouldn't hurt her French accent, either. Miss Lefebvre's is so very charming."

Sophie felt the prickling heat of a blush rise from her chest to her cheeks. She was not only embarrassed by such an unexpected compliment but was also surprised that the earl would speak so frankly of family matters in public. She would have imagined that the Duke and Duchess of Compton would have every tutor that a daughter might need, in place to mold their offspring ready for their Coming Out.

"Gertrude is the very devil, and you know it," Charlotte reminded him. "Your poor parents have yet to find anyone who will stay long enough to have any impact on her. Both of you have been spoiled, your entire lives."

"I cannot say that I disagree," Lord Wycliffe said amiably. "They made up for their absence in our lives by ensuring we had everything we could possibly need – if nothing at all that we actually wanted."

"I haven't ever heard you complaining," William teased his friend.

"And you never will," Lord Wycliffe confirmed. "I like getting what I want, when I want it."

Everyone laughed. But Lord Wycliffe turned to Sophie. "I do mean it," he assured her. "Despite their absence – or perhaps because of it - my dear Mama and busy Papa are very particular in whom they employ, and only those of the highest caliber are deemed suitable. I am sure that they would be delighted to know that they might secure the services of Miss Sophie Lefebvre, companion to the dowager Lady Benton."

She bowed her head gently, not enjoying the feeling of all eyes in the room resting upon her. "Thank you, my Lord," she said softly. "You are most kind. I cannot deny that such a position would, indeed, be an honor, but I do believe I 'ave all I need here."

"Are you trying to steal my friend?" Charlotte asked, her eyes narrowing as she looked at the earl as if trying to make out his intentions.

"Certainly not," he protested. "How could I ever steal your friend from you? She is much too devoted to leave your side. I daresay, she will spend all her days in your company."

The others laughed, but Sophie did not. The earl's observation was startling. Did he truly think she would never leave Charlotte's side? That she would spend the rest of her days in this house? Much as she loved Charlotte, and the home she had made here at Watton house, the suggestion she might never leave it was somewhat disconcerting, as if he were confirming her own beliefs that a marriage was most certainly impossible – and that she had no place anywhere else. A heavy breath left her lungs as she sipped at her mulled wine. She had tried, for so long, to resist the melancholy thoughts that reminded her of her situation, but now, as she sat amidst the happy faces of the Watts family, she couldn't deny them.

"Sophie, will you read to me?" George asked her, squeezing between her and the Earl of Wycliffe on the window seat.

"Of course, George," she said, pulling him closer, glad

of the distraction. She may not have children of her own, but she loved George and Emily dearly. It would be enough. It had to be.

The rest of the evening passed without incident. When the time came, Sophie took the children up to bed, exhausted and fractious after all the excitement of company. She was glad of a few moments away from those around her. She had never felt so alone since she'd become Charlotte's companion. Things had so clearly changed now, and she could no longer deny it to herself.

As she made her way back downstairs, she encountered the Earl of Wycliffe in the corridor. "Miss Lefebvre, might I speak with you, just for a moment," he said earnestly.

"Of course, my Lord," she said, though she didn't feel comfortable at all in this tiny space, alone with him. He was a very handsome man, and as he had confessed earlier was used to getting his own way. He had charisma and charm – and was just the kind of man that might pose a danger to someone such as Sophie.

He stepped closer and met her gaze. His dark brown eyes were mesmerizing. "Miss Lefebvre, I wish to sincerely apologize for my comments earlier. It was wrong of me to suggest that you might not be needed here any longer. I know you have been a true friend to Lady Watts for many years, and that she would never wish to be parted from you."

"I hope so, but you were not entirely wrong," Sophie admitted. "Lady Charlotte has little need of a companion, these days."

"I have seen Lady Charlotte blossom, since you came

into her life," Lord Wycliffe said sincerely. "My sister has need of that. I am her brother, and I do my best, but there are some things for which a woman is better equipped." Sophie smiled. He suddenly seemed so awkward. English men, she had noticed, were not good at expressing their emotions, or matters linked to them. It was rather endearing to see the suave and sophisticated earl so ill-at-ease.

"In all deference to my friends and the good home which they have given you, Miss Lefebvre, should you ever decide that you wished to take a new position, I would be delighted if you might consider us. Gertrude has need of someone just like you."

Sophie could not hide her look of surprise. She had thought he was merely jesting earlier, but it seemed that he truly meant what he had said. It was certainly something that she would need to consider – as it was becoming more and more clear to Sophie that she could not remain here, at Watton House, indefinitely.

"Wycliffe, the carriage is waiting," William called as he emerged into the corridor.

"I must go. Good night, Miss Lefebvre," Lord Wycliffe said, bowing to her politely before he turned and followed William and Mary, and the Duke of Mormont outside into the cool December night. Sophie watched him go, his words repeating in her mind.

"What did he want?" Charlotte asked as she joined Sophie at the door to wave their guests off. "He seemed quite intense."

"Nothing," Sophie replied, forcing a smile as the carriage rumbled away.

Her friend chuckled. "Claveston St. John has always been an odd one," she said with a good-natured smile as she shut the door and the two women headed upstairs to bed. "Good night, Sophie."

Sophie smiled. "Good night, Charlotte."

CHAPTER ONE

Six months later, Watton House

The wind howled around the estate, making the glass rattle in the windowpanes and loose doors clatter. The household staff rushed to secure them and to close the inner shutters in many of the rooms, to protect the inhabitants should the wind get strong enough to start breaking the glass. Thunder clapped loud enough to shake the casement windows, the lightning sending jagged fingers of light across the sky, illuminating the distant woods.

Sophie stood by the window in the parlor, resisting closing the shutters as she watched the gale as it ripped trees from their roots and buffeted everything in its path. She placed her hand on the glass, the tremble rippling through her palm as the thunder rolled once more. The very environment was alive.

"It's quite a storm," Charlotte said, peering over Sophie's shoulder, then returned to her spot by the fire.

"Indeed," Sophie replied and turned just enough to flash Charlotte a smile and see her take her fractious daughter from Mrs. Watts' arms. Charlotte sang softly to the baby, the child's soft coos barely audible between the performances of the raging storm. George burst into the room, grinning from ear to ear, and joined her at the window. Sophie gently smoothed his curls as they watched the roiling mass of grey clouds as it rumbled on overhead.

Both George and Emily were lovely children and Sophie adored them equally. But in recent days she felt further and further away from the family she had once considered herself a part of. It had become quite clear to Sophie, as she'd watched from the edges of every gathering throughout the long month of Christmas festivities, that she was on the outside.

Sophie still addressed both Charlotte and William with their titles when they were in company other than the direct family, as was fit and proper for her to do so. Yet, she couldn't help feeling that such formality would not be required if she was truly a friend and not a companion, Charlotte or William would be sufficient. She knew that she was permitted the license of calling them by their first names when in private, because of the closeness of their bond, yet it had come to hurt that those formalities were still necessary elsewhere.

"I should almost be afraid to stand near that window, Sophie," Mrs. Watts admitted, as she picked up her embroidery. "I would be afraid of the dead branches from the oak flying through it. Can you not close the shutters now?"

"It isn't as bad as that, my dear," Mr. Watts assured his wife, though he didn't once look up from his chess game. He and Captain Watts had been engaged in a game for the better part of an hour with no clear winner in sight.

Mrs. White, George's nurse entered the parlor looking flustered. "Oh, I am sorry, my Lady," she huffed. "I didn't realize he was here with you. I've been looking for him everywhere. As soon as the thunder started, he bolted."

"It's quite all right, Mrs. White," Charlotte assured the kindly older woman. "We all know George's feeling about storms. He will be quite fine here. You may have some time to yourself. He'll be quite safe with his dear Aunt Sophie," Charlotte assured her with a grin. "They share a morbid fascination for destruction." Mrs. White nodded and excused herself with a bobbed curtsey.

"Come here, my boy," Captain Watts called to his son, patting his knee. George looked up at Sophie, then at his father. "Come on, sit with me. I'll teach you a new game to pass the time while the storm rages."

"May I not count the lightning with Aunt Sophie?" George countered.

"You may," Captain Watts said, but looked genuinely saddened that George did not wish to join him.

"The storm will last some time. Perhaps we can count the lightning and thunder later?" Sophie urged the small boy. Her encouragement seemed to work. "Your father doesn't often 'ave the time to teach you chess, you'd best make the most of it." James laughed at her teasing and rose from his seat. Crossing the room in a few short strides, he collected his stepson and carried him back to the game with him.

They were a beautiful family, and Sophie envied them. God forgive her, but she did. She wished that it could be her life - but it wasn't and never would be. She was twenty-eight. The time for her to have such things was long past. "Do excuse me," she said, moving away from the window and towards the door.

"Are you quite well, Sophie?" Charlotte asked kindly.

"Very well," Sophie assured her, though she felt suddenly very cold and alone. "I need to write to my father."

"Please, send him and all of your family our regards as always," Charlotte replied.

Sophie smiled wanly. Her father and Charlotte were on fond terms after a single meeting some years previously. He would be delighted to know that Charlotte had been considerate enough to send her regards. "Certainly."

Once in her room, Sophie closed the door, leaning against the back of it as she tried to catch her breath. It was becoming more and more difficult to be around the family she loved, and it pained her that she should feel that way. She paced up and down the length of the large and comfortable room. She had been Charlotte's companion for nine wonderful years. Yet, she could no longer bear seeing her friend enjoy everything that she never would.

Christmas Eve and Lord Wycliffe's unexpected offer had popped into her thoughts in recent weeks more often than she cared to admit. She had not really been considering a change at that point, but as the days had passed, it had become an option with more and more merit. She walked toward her desk and took a seat. The paper and pen lay on the desktop, staring at her imposingly. Was she really considering this? She folded her hands in her lap and waited for a sign.

The thunder clapped overhead. She closed her eyes and took a deep breath, then reached for the pen. She wrote, letting everything she'd been thinking and everything she'd experienced in the past few weeks flood out of her, like it could be washed away with the pouring rain. Then she screwed up every page and burned them in the fire, before starting over. This time, she wrote concisely. She stared at the few lines on the page, wondering if it were really all as simple as this short and perfunctory letter made such a change out to be. The tears she couldn't stop crying told her it was not.

~

FIVE WEEKS LATER, Sophie was delivered of a letter confirming that she would be joining Lord Wycliffe's family at Compton Hall. She would assume the role of companion to his fourteen-year-old sister, Lady Gertrude. The compensation his father, the Duke of Compton, had offered was considerable and Sophie was unsure that she deserved such an increase to her income. But she knew that the Duke of Compton believed in paying what was deserved, so she took the figure stated to be a confirmation that the duke thought she was up to the task ahead.

Lord Wycliffe had unexpectedly neat handwriting. Sophie had expected it to be as flamboyant as the man himself, but it was considered, measured, and had barely a smudge upon the page. She tried to image Lord Wycliffe concentrating as he labored over the tiny letters and found herself smiling.

Yet it was still hard to believe that she would soon be leaving Watton House. That was all too real. The agreement was made. And there was only one thing left to do – to tell Charlotte. Sophie swallowed the lump in her throat. How could she possibly explain, without it seeming like a betrayal of their friendship - especially coming out of the blue, as such a declaration must surely seem.

Feeling unsettled, yet resolute, Sophie made her way down to the drawing-room, where Charlotte would be waiting for her. They had shared tea together at four o'clock in the drawing-room ever since Sophie had first come to Alnerton, and they had continued to meet each day after the move from Caldor House to Watton Hall. It would be just one of the little rituals that Sophie would miss terribly.

"There you are," Charlotte said, smiling. "I was about to have Mrs. Boyle call you."

Sophie was glad she had made it down before such a thing had occurred. The Watts' housekeeper was kind but could be very stern about timekeeping. "I am sorry," Sophie said with regret as she took her seat across from Charlotte. The tea was already prepared, steam rising from a fine China pot, an assortment of cakes and sandwiches on the tray beside it.

"You are barely a few minutes past time," Charlotte replied with a smile. "I was only teasing you. Is everything quite alright with you, dear Sophie? You've been terribly distracted in recent weeks."

"I am quite well," Sophie replied with a heavy heart, saddened to know that she hadn't kept her secrets perhaps as well as she thought she had. Charlotte had always been perceptive.

"I am glad," Charlotte replied, though her eyes didn't leave Sophie's face for a moment, seeking something she wasn't sure of – yet knew she would find if she just looked closely enough. "You do know you can tell me anything, don't you? You are family, and I always want what is best for you."

Charlotte poured the tea. Sophie reached for Charlotte's hand, stopping her in mid-pour. "Don't."

"So, there is something?" Charlotte said, her voice concerned, as she set the teapot back in its place.

"Yes," Sophie replied, swallowing her guilt like a bitter tonic.

"Are you unwell?" Charlotte scrutinized her appearance. "You look a little pale. Perhaps you should lay down. We can have tea tomorrow."

"No," Sophie answered. "I am very well. It is... it is just that I 'ave something to tell you, that I am afraid, will not make you 'appy."

Charlotte's brow furrowed, her concern seeming to grow by the minute. "What could you have to say that would make me unhappy? You can tell me anything. I would never judge you - you do know that don't you?

Whatever it is, nothing will change between us, I am certain of it."

Sophie could hardly look at Charlotte. The inside of her mouth was as dry as the desert, and her mind seemed to falter on the words she had practiced so often, since receiving the confirmation letter from Lord Wycliffe. She pursed her lips and wrung her hands in her lap, wondering how she could possibly tell Charlotte the truth.

"Sophie? You're worrying me," Charlotte said softly, reaching a hand over the table and taking Sophie's. She squeezed it tightly. "Whatever is the matter?"

Sophie lifted her emerald eyes to her friend's face. "I'm sorry," she whispered.

"Sorry? For what?"

"For telling you this way, that I shall be leaving here in little under a fortnight to take up a new position."

Charlotte's eyes widened. "Leave here? Why? Have I done something to upset you? Has somebody else?"

"No. It is not that. You must never think anyone here could ever be unkind," Sophie pleaded. She couldn't bear it if Charlotte thought that she was in the wrong for being so happy.

"Then what? What would you make you leave here?"

Sophie shook her head. "I love you, Charlotte, as I would a sister. I could 'ave asked for no one better to act as a companion to." She paused and took a deep breath. "But you no longer need a companion. You 'ave Capitaine James, and his family now. You 'ave Mrs. White to care for George and Emily with you, and Mrs. Boyle to run the household. You 'ave Mr. and

Mrs. Watts who are delighted to 'ave you and the children."

"But I still need you," Charlotte said, tears beginning to pool in her lovely eyes.

"Dearest Charlotte, I shall always be your friend, and will gladly write often – and would be delighted to visit when my new employers might permit that. You will not lose me, not entirely."

"But you will not be here. You know, I have feared that this day might come. I have so much less time now, and you are right, that my needs are different now. You must get bored sometimes. Are you terribly unhappy?"

"Sometimes," Sophie admitted. "I thought I could be 'appy to watch you have your love story come true. I wanted nothing more than for you and Capitaine James to find one another once more. Yet, I find, that your joy has left me to wonder about my own happiness."

Charlotte's voice was tainted with sadness. "Why did you not say? I would never want you to be unhappy, Sophie. I love you. I want your happiness as much as my own."

"I love you too, Charlotte. That is why I could never say it out loud. I did not want to spoil your 'appiness. I 'ave been blessed to watch it, as much as it 'urt me to see it."

"I don't fully understand," Charlotte said, "but I want to."

"I want what you 'ave, Charlotte," Sophie admitted. It felt strange to say it out loud. It had been something she had only ever thought about in the privacy of her own mind. It was strangely freeing to hear her own voice confessing to her deepest and most treasured secret. "I want a husband, children, my own home," Sophie answered. "But I can never 'ave it and that is sometimes painful for me, when I see you so very content."

Charlotte's tears were now flowing freely over her cheeks. "Oh, Sophie. But such a thing is so easy for us to change. There are plenty of eligible men who would love a wife as pretty and accomplished as you."

"If I were perhaps ten years younger, or even five," Sophie said drily, rolling her eyes. They both knew that hope for a good marriage was gone for her now. "No, I must accept that is not to be my path and so, I 'ave found a new position," Sophie said briskly. She did not wish to cry, though she was struggling not to.

"But must you truly leave so soon?" Charlotte asked. "A fortnight is barely enough time for us to make our goodbyes after all this time."

Sophie shook her head. "I'm sorry, Charlotte. Perhaps that it is so sudden is for the best."

Her friend sprung to her feet. "But where are you going?"

"To the Duke of Compton, at Compton Hall."

"You're going to Compton?" Charlotte asked incredulously.

"Lord Wycliffe offered me a position at Christmas," Sophie explained.

"It was a joke," Charlotte said, her eyes flashing with what looked like anger.

"No, it was not," Sophie corrected. "He meant every word, and I shall be Gertrude's companion. The contract is signed."

"Sophie, please," Charlotte cried. "What will I do without you?"

Sophie gave her dearest friend a sad smile. "You will continue to be 'appy, my dear Charlotte. I will write to you if you will let me. I would like to maintain our friendship."

Her stomach tightened. What if the end of her service meant the end of their friendship as well?

"What will I tell James and children? The entire household will miss you so dreadfully."

"Should I tell them myself?" Sophie questioned.

Charlotte dabbed her eyes with a lace-trimmed handkerchief. "No, I think it better come from me. I am sure they will have questions. You would have to endure this again. Could you bear that?"

Sophie swallowed hard. "I do not think I could. This 'as been so much 'arder than anything I have ever had to do – and much worse than I imagined it might be."

"How long have you known you were leaving?"

"I only received the final confirmation of my employment in a letter from Lord Wycliffe, just today," Sophie divulged. Charlotte was quiet. "Are you angry?" Sophie asked.

"Not at all," Charlotte replied. "I'm saddened, but not angry. You have never made me angry in the nine years we have been together. I very much doubt you could make me angry now."

Sophie stood and the two friends embraced. "So, now we must make every moment you are here count," Charlotte said trying to sound brave. "Not a single chance wasted."

"Oui! Whatever you wish," Sophie said forcing herself to sound as cheerful as she possibly could. "I am at your disposal."

"You are my very best friend, Sophie Lefebvre. I will miss you so dearly that I cannot find words."

"As I will miss you, Charlotte."

"I wish you every happiness, Sophie."

Sophie knew that she would miss Charlotte and Watton House terribly, but new adventures awaited her at Compton Hall. Gertrude was a young girl on the cusp of womanhood. Sophie looked forward to helping her become a fine young woman. Charlotte had already been well situated in life and experience by the time Sophie had entered her life. Sophie had offered little more than companionship and understanding, during her years of loss, but Gertrude was a chance for Sophie to make a difference. She would focus on that in the weeks to come. It would make the pending separation easier.

Charlotte grinned at her and took her seat at the table once more. "Shall we have tea now?"

Sophie smiled and sat back down opposite her. "I'll pour."

CHAPTER TWO

Compton Hall, Hertfordshire

The image staring back at Claveston St. John was that of a fine figure of a man. The new green velvet jacket and matching silk waistcoat went well with his cream breeches and new silk cravat. He'd heard others call him a dandy, and he didn't mind that. Clothes made the man, did they not? And if so, his were made by the finest tailor in London, of the best fabrics. Beau Brummel himself would be proud to cut such a dashing figure.

Claveston was determined to make the best impression on Miss Sophie Lefebvre upon her arrival, and there was no expense too great for that. He smoothed his black hair and ran a hand over his sideburns to ensure they were neat. An unkempt appearance was hardly suitable for a first meeting, and that was what Claveston considered this to be, despite having met Miss Lefebvre before. This was a new start.

"Mrs. Grint, has there been any sign of a carriage?"

"No," the doughty housekeeper said, looking him up and down and rolling her eyes with amusement. "But they'll be here soon enough." Claveston chose to ignore the impertinence. Mrs. Grint had been with the family for longer than he could remember. She had never seemed to grow any older in that time, or perhaps he had simply frozen her image. He would never know – but she had been the one constant in his life, and he was very fond of her.

Compton Hall had been built by Claveston's grandfather. It had more than forty rooms, including four drawing rooms - so that at least one might get the best of the sun at any time of day or year. It was surrounded by acres of parkland and woodlands for hunting, all landscaped in the latest style. At least one wing of the vast mansion was always being re-decorated at any time, as Mama liked to keep up with the latest fashions, though she was barely ever present to enjoy the fruits of her imagination.

Claveston felt peculiarly invigorated today, as he headed towards the only drawing room with a view out over the long and winding driveway from the road to the hall. A grin played on his lips as he thought of Miss Lefebvre's arrival. Ever since her first letter, he had looked forward to the moment when he would be able to introduce her to his family and show her his home. It had been of little moment to get his father to agree to her coming, after all the hall and the estate would one day be his, and Papa was rarely present to know who worked for him.

This particular drawing-room was decorated in a more manly fashion than the others, and so Claveston tended to use it, even when the sun wasn't kind enough to bless it with full and glorious light. Gold damask wallpaper adorned the drawing-room walls, which were covered with large paintings of Claveston's many accomplished and intriguing ancestors. A large, patterned carpet covered the entire floor. Father had brought it back from one of his many trips overseas. It had cost a small fortune and had been the envy of *the Ton* when it had arrived.

There were four doors into the room: one from the cavernous hallway, where a grand staircase wound up from either side of the hallway, meeting at a wide balcony at the first floor; another from the Yew Room, which was a library filled with marquetry work done by the finest craftsmen; one from his father's study; and french doors that led outside onto a terrace with an ornamental stone balustrade.

Claveston collected the book he'd left on the table beside the sofa and sat down, crossed his legs and relaxed back to read. The sofa, like the other upholstered furniture in this room was all covered with black velvet, with embroidery in gold thread to match the wallpaper. It could have been ostentatious, gauche even – but Mama's exquisite taste somehow made it seem tasteful and opulent.

The room was filled with all kinds of odd trinkets, pieces of furniture, and oddments that his father had brought home from his travels. A beautifully painted armoire from China to a cigar box from France, a silver thimble to a huge, turning globe that sat untouched in the corner of the room. Nobody but Papa had any real desire to travel and see the world, and so when he pointed to the places he'd been, his family feigned interest but didn't really care.

Claveston tried to focus on what he was reading but gave up after repeating the same sentence several times. His mind was simply too preoccupied. He set the book aside and walked out onto the terrace to see if there was any sign of the carriage. There was not. He checked his pocket watch and noted that Miss Lefebvre was fifteen minutes past due. He tutted under his breath and paced a little to try and get rid of some of his restless energy.

Taking a deep breath, he raised his face to the sun and closed his eyes. It was a refreshing day, with bright sunshine and just a hint of a cooling breeze. It was the perfect weather for traveling. Miss Lefebvre should have been early, not late, on a day such as this.

The doors clicked behind him and before he could turn around, he felt the slender arms of his sister, Gertrude, wrap around his middle. "Claveston," she declared happily as he turned and embraced her warmly.

"Gertrude," he said, laughing. "You would think you have not seen me in a year, and not simply overnight, you must learn to curb your delight in seeing me. I do not deserve it."

"Am I too excited?" Gertrude said brightly, turning slightly so she might peer down the driveway as well. "I cannot help it. Miss Lefebvre comes today, and I can hardly wait to meet her."

"I am glad you are so pleased about it," Claveston said with a wry smile. Gertrude was rarely happy about any new attempt to curb her more boisterous ways. She had gone out of her way to upset and drive off more nannies and governesses than Claveston wished to count.

"Oh, thank you so much for finding her for me," Gertrude continued. "It is the most wonderful gift to have a companion of my own. All of the girls of my acquaintance have one, but Miss Lefebvre will be the most wonderful of them all, as she is more accomplished than all of their companions put together."

There was a certain joy that came from making his sister happy. He'd spent most of his life with that sole motivation. Their parents, generous and loving as they were, often had other things to occupy them - and were often far away when their children needed them most.

When he was a boy, Claveston had indulged himself in their gifts and the company of the boys at school. The friendships he had made with people like James and William had seen him through some tough times, and their friendships would last his entire life. But Gertrude didn't have such a luxury. Young women did not go away to school or university as he had. For her, nannies and governesses had come and gone, citing one reason or another for their departure, most saying that Gertrude was too unruly and that there was nothing more they might do to help her.

His sister was a wonderful girl but had been too often left alone. Where school and university had given Claveston structure and rules, Gertrude had grown up spoiled and inclined to have her own way. She was more than a little stubborn, but all she truly longed for was to be loved. Claveston prayed with all his heart that Miss Lefebvre would not only give her a guide into woman-hood but that she would also become Gertrude's friend and confidante, as she was with Charlotte. Gertrude needed that more than anything.

"I'm glad you are pleased with my choice. I hope you will be even more so once you meet her."

"How could I not be when you have chosen her?" Gertrude said, looking up at him with a grin. "My brother has the most wonderful taste of anyone I know."

He chuckled. "You flatter me, Gertrude."

"I do not. Whatever I say about you is true," she protested, pouting slightly. It was a habit she had recently acquired, and Claveston had to admit he wasn't delighted by it.

Yet, her insistence made him smile. "I hope others will think the same."

"Who wouldn't?" she asked, glancing around as if they might be present and she intended to give them a piece of her mind. Claveston chuckled. "Tell me who they are, and I shall set them straight."

He would never confide it to anyone, much less his little sister, but his interest in Miss Lefebvre was not solely for Gertrude's benefit. He did not wish for anyone to think that he might have brought Miss Lefebvre to Compton for his own purposes. It would do little for her reputation - and when he had first made the offer it had been far from the truth. His most sincere desire had been for Gertrude to have a friend who could be as close to her as Miss Lefebvre was to Charlotte.

Yet, as they had swapped letters, to arrange her appointment, Claveston had come to know Miss Levebvre in a different way. She was modest and good - and had little understanding of her value to his family. Claveston's mind filled with the cursive strokes her pen made against the page in her letters. She had a delicate hand, which matched her spirit. She had such controlled elegance, such grace, and poise. She was one of the most understated women amongst his acquaintance. Yet she stood out in a room filled with Society beauties.

"Why do you smile so?" Gertrude's question interrupted his contemplation, and Claveston woke himself from his musing.

"Nothing."

His sister frowned. "Not nothing. I have never seen you smile in that way. Something must be the cause of it. What is it?"

"Lord Claveston," Mrs. Grint interrupted, stepping out onto the terrace. "Cooper has returned from the village with news. The carriage passed through Compton several minutes ago and is now on the hall road. It should be here within minutes."

Claveston breathed a sigh of relief and was unable to stop himself from smiling. "There, you smiled like that again, Claveston," Gertrude noted with a teasing grin.

"Don't be ridiculous, Gertrude. There is nothing curious about my smile," he said dismissively. "Thank you, Mrs. Grint. That will be all." The housekeeper gave him a look, but she left without a word.

Gertrude's brow remained furrowed as she stared at him. He smoothed her forehead with his thumb. "Come now, you don't want wrinkles before you find a husband, do you?" he teased. "Your special guest has almost arrived. We should go to greet her," he urged, taking her by the arm and escorting her to the entrance.

His steps were brisk at first, but he slowed them purposefully. He didn't want anyone to think he was excited. He was not a schoolboy who became energized by the visits of strangers. He was the Earl of Wycliff, a gentleman, and he had control over himself.

As they reached the front door, Claveston could see the carriage coming up the drive; a light cloud of dust rose from the horses' hoofs as they progressed up the gravel path. Gertrude held his arm tightly as he escorted her down the grand stone staircase onto the driveway to meet her new companion.

Gertrude looked at him curiously, but he ignored it. His sister was often too curious, but there was no need for concern. Soon, she would have all the entertainment she needed and would find him less fascinating.

He had been her anchor, throughout her short life. Whilst he had been away at school and university it had been difficult for her, being surrounded by mostly servants. He knew, if Gertrude would let her, that Miss Lefebvre could become someone that his sister could turn to and rely upon. She needed someone to guide her through the trials and tribulations of young womanhood – something he most certainly could not do.

He couldn't deny, that having someone like Miss Lefebvre here with Gertrude would also make his life easier, too. Though he often acted as if his life was all about fun, his sister was never far from his mind. When he was gone, she was alone, and he was aware of that, and it troubled him, which was why he never stayed away long, but instead enjoyed frequent visits to divide himself between his own more selfish pursuits and to ensure Gertrude's happiness.

The carriage crunched to a halt. Claveston rushed to the door, opened it, and held out his hand. "Miss Lefebvre, welcome."

A slender, gloved hand slipped into his palm, and Claveston felt his back straighten and his chest lift as she stepped down from the coach and met his gaze. "Lord Wycliffe," she said, dipping her head to look at the ground and offering him a polite curtsey as soon as her feet touched the floor.

A quick glance at his sister, who was stood a few steps back at the bottom of the stairs, to see if she had noticed how gracefully Miss Lefebvre had got down from the carriage told him she had. Her eyes were wide with admiration. Claveston stepped back and bowed. "I trust your trip was a pleasant one," he said, offering her his arm.

"It was not unenjoyable," she replied with a delicate smile. "Perhaps a little longer than I expected."

They walked towards Gertrude who dropped into a slightly clumsy curtsey. "Please, allow me to present my sister, Lady Gertrude St. John. Gertrude, this is Miss Lefebvre, your new companion."

"Miss Lefebvre." Gertrude gave an awkward smile.

"Lady Gertrude, it is a pleasure," Sophie replied with a much broader one. "I look forward to getting to know you well. I 'ave looked forward to this day for some weeks now."

"As have I," Gertrude said excitedly.

"I am sure you both will be fast friends in no time at all," Claveston said hopefully.

CHAPTER THREE

"Shall we go in? I've arranged for some refreshments, and I wish to show you the house," Claveston said eagerly.

"I look forward to it," Miss Lefebvre said as she looked up at the vast edifice of the mansion in front of her, her eyes wide. "Though I fear it is much larger than anything I am used to. Even Caldor was not so grand." She turned to Gertrude and smiled. "Lady Gertrude, you will 'ave to make sure I do not get lost."

"It has more than forty rooms," Gertrude said proudly, obviously delighted that Miss Lefebvre had included her. "It will take some time for you to get used to it, but in a few weeks, I am sure you will find your way."

"The servants will carry your things to your suite," Claveston added as Miss Lefebvre looked back to the carriage where her trunk was being unloaded. "We have given you the whole of the west wing on the second floor, as your private accommodation."

"That is too much," Miss Lefebvre protested. "I am quite content with just a single room in the attic."

"Your rooms are next to mine," Gertrude said happily. "And Claveston's suite is right next to the rooms that my grandfather had prepared for the King, should he ever visit us here at Compton. My father is a cousin or something to King George. There is a marble bust in the great hall that is an exact likeness of His Majesty."

Miss Lefebvre smiled at the girl's enthusiasm. Claveston tried not to be put out, but it seemed that she was reserving all of her attentions for his sister, and none for him. Had he done something wrong? Usually, the ladies of his acquaintance hung on his every word, however banal, and were always eager to see the estate he would one day inherit. His family were amongst the most influential in England, his father had acted as an advisor to King George and continued to serve the Prince Regent.

However, Miss Lefebvre seemed disinterested in the wealth and status of his family. He took that to heart. Such things might not impress her, but he was sure that there would be something that might. And he reminded himself, Miss Lefebvre had already made his acquaintance. She had yet to meet Gertrude and was here to be his sister's companion. It was only fair that he let them become better known to one another, much as he wished to monopolize Miss Lefebvre's attentions.

"Shall I show you to your suite so you might freshen up after your journey?" he asked her.

She looked hesitant but hooked her arm in his. "Thank you, I should like that."

"Gertrude?" Claveston said, offering his other arm to his sister. She took it, and the trio went inside. Claveston introduced Sophie to Mrs. Grint and Bonnet, the butler, who awaited her arrival in the hallway, before proceeding upstairs to Miss Lefebvre's rooms. The walk took several minutes.

"Your new home," Claveston said, flinging open the painted double doors to the suite as they arrived. A spacious parlor with elegant French furniture lay behind them. Miss Lefebvre gasped, her beautiful green eyes wide with delight as she took in the pale colors and almost floor-to ceiling windows that flooded the room with light.

Gertrude grabbed her hand and dragged her to the windows. "You can see the whole park from your balcony," she said, wrenching the door open and pulling Miss Lefebvre outside.

"It is quite spectacular," Miss Lefebvre sighed.

"And you have a dressing room, and a bedroom, and there is a room for a lady's maid, though you do not have one," Gertrude added excitedly as they came back inside.

"Thank you, Lord Wycliffe," Miss Lefebvre said with a tired smile. "This is so much more than I need."

"I just hope you will be comfortable here," he said softly.

"Yes, well, if you would excuse me," she said a little awkwardly. "But perhaps I should unpack."

"Will you join us for some refreshments on the terrace?" Gertrude asked her eagerly. "I would love you to join us, Miss Lefebvre. It was done especially for you."

"Then how can I refuse?" Miss Lefebvre replied. "I will be down shortly."

"I will take Gertrude down and return for you," Claveston said swiftly, reaching for his sister, before she tried to inveigle an invite to stay. It was quite clear that Miss Lefebvre needed a moment alone to compose herself.

"That will not be necessary. I think I can remember the way back downstairs."

"It would be my pleasure."

"Please, my Lord, I 'ave already taken up so much of your time. I know you are a busy man."

"Very well," he replied, trying to hide his disappointment. "If you ring the bell at your bedside someone will come up to you, or there is bound to be someone in the hall who will point you in the right direction."

"Thank you," Miss Lefebvre said with a polite smile. Claveston bowed as he nudged his sister out of the room.

He walked with Gertrude back to the terrace, trying not to feel put out by the way in which his attempts to please Miss Lefebvre seemed to have failed. Why did she not see the trouble he had gone to? He could name a hundred young women in Society who would have been delighted to be presented with such a suite of rooms – and they weren't here as servants.

"Is something wrong, Claveston?" Gertrude asked him, looking up at him curiously. "You look strange?"

"No, nothing is wrong, Gertrude," he assured her.

"You're lying. You said you would never lie to me," his sister replied frankly.

He sighed. He hated it when she caught him out. "I'm sorry. You're right. I am not being truthful, but I assure you, it is nothing of consequence. I was just wondering how else we could make Miss Lefebvre feel at home. She's been with Lady Charlotte for so long I expect her new surroundings will take some getting used to. I wish to make it easier for her, that is all."

Gertrude smiled. "May I help? I want Miss Lefebvre to enjoy her time here as well. I am sure if we work together, we can make a glorious plan."

∼

THE FIRST DAYS at Compton Hall were more difficult than Sophie had expected. When she recalled the early days of her time with Charlotte, she did not recall them being so fraught with concerns. She could not even blame anyone else for her feelings of disquiet now. It was no fault of the family, as only Lord Wycliffe and Lady Gertrude were here and both were endlessly kind to her; nor was it a problem with the staff, as they were all very agreeable. The fault lay within her. She missed Charlotte, and Emily and George - and the family she had left behind at Watton House. She missed the ease of her old life.

Everything that Lord Wycliffe had done to make her feel at home, actually did the opposite. The luxurious suite of rooms he had prepared for her, so she might have some freedom and privacy only served to add to her loneliness. The space was too great, and though Gertrude was in the suite next door, that was still some way away, and she couldn't hear a peep from her, no matter how loudly the girl carried on. The good-natured hustle and bustle of Watton House seemed so very far away.

Her nights at Compton were filled with contemplation, the incessant wondering if she'd made the right choice in coming here. Perhaps she had made a terrible mistake? Perhaps she should have held her tongue and persevered against her feelings, in time surely her jealousy would have faded? But it was too late now. She couldn't go backwards. Her only hope was to move onwards and to make the best of her new life.

Every morning, Sophie brushed through her long dark hair, the ends curling in her hand as she smoothed it through, then pinned it carefully. Gertrude would wake at around eight o'clock, and Sophie needed to be ready long before that. She had always liked to write in her journal before going about the day, and that habit gave a little piece of normalcy in her completely changed world. It gave her time to reflect on her life and where it was going.

She sat at her desk and just wrote. She poured every feeling, every thought onto the page. How lost and alone she felt - and how she missed Charlotte and George, and little Emily. She wondered what they were doing now that she was gone. Were they enjoying themselves or did they miss her as much as she missed them?

She often wrote for more than half an hour before the clock would chime, reminding her that she had her duties to perform. She would set the pen aside and hide the pages in her desk before locking it and heading from the room. Her journal was the only record of her unhappiness. Nobody else need ever know.

After breakfast, she and Gertrude would walk in the garden, talk, and get to know one another, before the young woman would attend her lessons in music, literature, and art – subjects deemed fitting for a young lady. During that time, Sophie had little to do but read, though Lord Wycliffe had given her full access to the house. Sophie did not feel comfortable wandering aimlessly through the many rooms. It felt too much like she was exploring other worlds, rather than getting to know her new home.

"Good morning Lady Gertrude," Sophie said as she entered the breakfast room. The young woman was sitting in her place at the table, a steaming cup of hot chocolate in front of her and a slice of seedcake upon her plate. "I do hope that you have had something other than that to sustain you."

"Miss Lefebvre, good morning," Lady Gertrude replied with a grin as Sophie helped herself to coddled eggs, crisp bacon, and a cup of coffee. "I have already had coddled eggs. They were quite delicious."

"The weather is very fine today. I thought we could walk through the orchard instead of the gardens today. What do you think?"

"It sounds wonderful," Lady Gertrude said excitedly. I haven't been to the orchards in some time. Though, I must confess I do prefer flowers to fruit," she added with a giggle.

Sophie smiled as she sat down. "I love them both. But when the weather is so fine, I just like to be outdoors."

She ate her repast in small, dainty bites. She was always conscious of showing her young charge a good example, and aware that every moment was one where she was teaching Lady Gertrude how to behave. She chewed and swallowed carefully, ensuring she had finished every morsel before she took a sip from her water glass or coffee cup, to ensure that she left no mark behind when she did.

Lady Gertrude tried to copy with her seed cake, and Sophie smiled warmly at her when she got it right, and just repeated something if she hadn't quite mastered it. When she was done, she rose from the table gracefully. "Shall we?"

The ladies fell into step beside one other. Lady Gertrude was rather diminutive, with small, delicate bones - unlike her tall and muscular brother. She had a trim waist and pretty hair that held a curl well. Her perfectly made gowns suited her beautifully, always in hues and patterns that most flattered her figure and her coloring. She had the makings of a fine young woman if she could just learn to be a little more demure and slightly less stubborn.

They made their way through the house and out onto the back terrace. The wide paved expanse overlooked the formal gardens. They walked along the neatly edged gravel pathways, smiling at the gardeners as they clipped the low hedges, in their crisp geometric shapes. They turned to the east, through the walled kitchen garden, and out to the vast orchards behind.

"Lady Gertrude, when will your parents be returning?" Sophie asked curiously as they sauntered between the apple and pear trees. She was surprised that she had yet to meet her new employers.

"Please, call me Gertrude. The servants call me Lady Gertrude and you are no servant," the young lady said breathlessly, then gave Sophie a scared look. "Should I have said that?" she asked anxiously.

"Of course, though it is often best to maintain formalities in social situations, when you go to London for your Season," Sophie said. "And I shall be delighted to call you Gertrude if you will call me Sophie."

"I should like that, Sophie," Gertrude said, savoring the name. "It is a very pretty name. Much nicer than Gertrude."

"Gertrude is quite distinguished," Sophie assured her. "It is a very strong name, for a strong young woman."

Gertrude flushed becomingly at the compliment. She ducked her head shyly as if unused to people being kind. "There, that is better. I much prefer that. My name sounds very different when you say it."

"It is my accent, per'aps," Sophie replied. She never heard her accent. In her mind, she sounded as she always had and it was those around her that had accents, but as the foreigner amongst the English, she knew the oddity was hers to bear.

"As to the whereabouts of Mama and Papa, I do not know when my parents will return." Gertrude's voice was tight, her eyes sad. "You would have to ask Claveston. He keeps abreast of their travels."

Sophie sighed. She had done her best to avoid Lord Wycliffe since her arrival. He was so kind and so keen for her to be happy that it had the opposite effect. Every

encounter at supper left her wishing for the easy infor-
mality she had shared with Charlotte and the Watts' in
Alnerton and made her long to go home. It wasn't so
important that she know when the duke and duchess
would return, though it was clear that Gertrude grew
more unhappy the longer they were gone.

Gertrude hooked her arm around Sophie's. "The day
is so lovely," she said brightly as if they had just been
speaking of the birds in the trees. Sophie was quite
disconcerted by how mercurial Gertrude's moods
could be.

"The orchard smells wonderful in the heat, doesn't
it?" Gertrude continued excitedly. "Thank you for
suggesting we walk here today. It is such a different
aroma to flowers. I should walk here more often."

Sophie forced herself to smile as they walked among
the apple blossom, though their conversation had given
her much to think upon. "We will be blessed with cherry
blossom, and plum in the coming weeks," she said to
Gertrude. "In a few months, these trees will be filled with
fruits and will need to be thinned so only the healthiest
are left to ripen on the boughs."

"How do you know?"

"I have always liked gardens. In Alnerton I questioned the gardeners very often. They were always
willing to answer me. I learned a lot there."

"You miss it."

"It is to be expected. I did not leave because of ill-
treatment. On the contrary, they treated me very well.
Like family."

"Then why did you come here?" Gertrude asked, full of youthful curiosity.

Sophie smiled. "Lady Charlotte has her family. She does not need my company. You do."

Gertrude flung her arms around her waist and hugged her tightly. "This is so wonderful. I couldn't have asked for anything better."

CHAPTER FOUR

"Where in France are you from, Sophie?" Gertrude asked a few days later, as she walked up and down the length of the long gallery, with three heavy books balanced upon her head. She was surprisingly good at it and the exercise was improving her posture as Sophie intended it to.

In the past weeks since her arrival, the two women had shared little about each other. But it seemed that the early awkwardness had passed since their walk together in the orchards. Such difficulties were to be expected. Gertrude was fifteen years Sophie's junior, and the age gap had left Sophie a little lost for topics of conversation. It had been some time since she'd felt the flush of youth, the excitement of becoming a debutante, so she was glad that Gertrude now felt able to ask more personal questions – and that she did not mind answering them.

"I was born in Montauban, in the south of France. It has been many years since I 'ave been there," she admitted.

"Is your family still there?"

"Oui. My father is Baron Maurice Lefebvre."

"French gentry?" Gertrude questioned curiously as she turned at the end of the gallery and began to walk back towards Sophie. "I had no idea your father was of the French aristocracy. I presumed you were only a wealthy man's daughter."

Sophie smiled. "I am that also. These days, since La Revolution, it isn't so wise to be a nobleman. He would not ever use his title, though it is his, still, by right. When I was a tiny girl, we moved to Marseille, where my father recovered our family's lost fortunes by exporting fine linens from the region to countries such as Portugal, Spain and England."

Gertrude smiled at Sophie her eyes bright with the glow of youthful curiosity. "How fascinating. Do they visit you often? I would be pleased to make their acquaintance."

"My father is not fond of long voyages any longer. He and my mother have returned to Montauban and live a quiet life now."

"Do you have brothers and sisters at all?"

"No. I am an only child."

"Do you visit your parents?"

"No," Sophie answered, her heart heavy. "It is very expensive to travel so far. My life has been in England for many years. I do not venture home, but I do miss my family. I don't know how time flies by so quickly. One day it is just a week, the next years have gone by and you haven't seen your loved ones."

Gertrude nodded. "I understand. My parents are

always away. They never had time for me or Claveston. Since I was a girl, they have spent less than a quarter of any given year with me. My brother was always the one who cared for me."

Such a situation was not unusual. The life of the aristocracy in England was semi-nomadic at best, with time spent in London for the Season, summers in Bath or the country, and Christmas at their estates. From all Charlotte and William had told Sophie of the Duke and Duchess of Compton, they traveled more than most – as the duke liked to visit every single one of his family's holdings at least once a year, and the duchess enjoyed taking the waters at every spa in the country, as well as shopping trips around Europe to purchase her trinkets to decorate this vast home.

Regardless, it made Sophie sad. She had been blessed with the parents God had given her. They had been present to love and cherish her, and she knew that she was a better person for it. She placed a gentle hand on the young woman's shoulder. "Well, now, you have another person to care for you."

Gertrude's smile broadened. "Truly?"

Sophie nodded. "Truly." The girl's dark eyes shone with pleasure.

But the moment of closeness between them did not seem destined to last. A flicker of something passed across Gertrude's pretty face, and in an instant, the child she was seemed to have disappeared, replaced by a cynical and troubled woman. "Do you care for my brother?"

The question took Sophie by surprise. She frowned, unsure of what answer Gertrude might wish to hear. "What do you mean?"

"Have you come here in the hopes of making my brother your husband, or have you truly come here for me?"

The question was leveled with such candor that Sophie was momentarily unable to speak. But it was clear that this was a matter of the utmost importance to Gertrude. Lord Wycliffe was not a man Sophie had ever considered. Not once. He was entirely too interested in his wealth and consequence to be of any interest to her.

Indeed, his self-importance and arrogance were amongst the qualities that had given her concern when she first considered whether to take the position as Gertrude's companion. It had taken many days and nights of consideration to make the choice to take this position – and only once it had been clear that she was to be the duke's servant and not his son's.

She had yet to be proved incorrect about her assumptions, as since her arrival, the Earl of Wycliffe had proven himself to be even more consumed with his trappings than with things she considered more important. But she could also see now that he was a kind man, and obviously loved his sister dearly. He was witty and amusing, and excellent company at dinner – but in all honesty, she knew that she could reassure Gertrude that she had no intention of setting her cap at the girl's brother.

She looked Gertrude in the eye. "I have no interest in Lord Wycliffe, not in that manner."

Gertrude looked surprised. "Are you sure? Ladies always come here, pretending to be my friend, but they have no interest in me. Their interests are always in my brother."

Sophie chuckled. She could believe it. He was the type to attract a woman as shallow as he was. Poor girl. Sophie wondered how many would-be duchesses the poor child had been forced to endure? "I promise you. I have no interest in your brother. Lord Wycliffe is not the kind of man I would ever consider."

Her response seemed to please Gertrude, her smile grew wide. "Wonderful! Then I may look forward to finally having a real friend."

Sophie suspected that the question that had just been asked had been a fear lurking in Gertrude's mind that whole time, making it even harder for them to truly become better acquainted. If Gertrude had been questioning Sophie's motives, that might explain why things had often been a little strained between them before. Hopefully, that was behind them now.

"Do you have many friends?" Sophie asked, knowing she was testing the bounds of their new-found accord.

"Mama and Papa always wanted the best company for me," Gertrude explained "They don't consider many girls, even the daughters of their own peers, to be our equal. Claveston was lucky, though they were choosy about his acquaintances, too, he left to attend school where he made friends of his own."

"And you have just had governesses and tutors?"

"And no matter how kind they may be, such people can never be friends," Gertrude said sadly. "They were only here for a wage. My nannies all left to marry. The only person who has ever stayed is Claveston."

"You need not worry about that now," Sophie assured her. "I came here to be with you."

The child returned; the dark cloud of the woman, old before her time, vanished as soon as she had arrived. Gertrude clapped her hands happily. "Oh, Sophie! We shall be the greatest of friends! We can paint together, go for walks, and have picnics. We shall have a marvelous time."

Sophie smiled. "Of course. And, if your family permits, I will accompany you when you 'ave your first Season."

"You will act as my chaperone when I Come Out?"

"To some extent, though a young woman is usually presented at Court by her mother or another close relative. But I shall accompany you to the card parties and soirees, the meeting rooms and the theatre – and the balls, of course."

Gertrude beamed at that. "I am a terrible dancer," she confessed.

"You will be an expert by the time we leave for London," Sophie assured her. "I will show you how the ladies of Society interact. How they carry themselves in company and make sure that you know the steps to every dance you might ever need to know."

"Thank you, Sophie. I already feel much more content about it, knowing you will be by my side."

"I am glad because someday soon, men will present themselves to you with regard to claiming your hand. You must always stake care of your reputation. Not every man is a gentleman."

Gertrude giggled. "I find it hard to believe that gentlemen will look at me, and consider me as a potential bride," she admitted. "I am only a girl."

"You are a young lady, Gertrude. And though that can be hard, by learning all I can teach you, you can arm yourself to bear it – and even enjoy it."

Gertrude listened with rapt attention her eyes glued to Sophie as she spoke. It was strange to direct one so young. Charlotte had never needed such guidance, she was already acquainted with the way of the world as she had a companion before, but Gertrude was different. She could see both the child and the young woman in her eyes. Gertrude was not yet experienced enough to handle the adult world, but she was not as naïve as some might think.

"You won't ever leave me, will you?" Gertrude said suddenly, her eyes wide with fear.

Sophie was silent. It was a question that a child might ask, one who could not see past their own needs, and Sophie did not wish to tell Gertrude a lie – but she also knew that the truth would be too hard for her to bear. It was impossible to say what the future might hold. She could not say, for definite, whether she might have to part with this fragile young woman someday.

"I beg your pardon, Sophie," Gertrude asked, looking down for a moment, before boldly holding Sophie's gaze once more. "I do not mean to offend, but I know you are older, much too old for a husband and children, therefore there will be no need for you to leave."

Sophie had not expected such a bald statement of her

circumstances from one so young. Taken aback, she responded without thinking. "No, I do not expect I will find a husband at my age."

"I am sorry," Gertrude said, though she did not look even the tiniest bit contrite. "But I am also glad, for my sake. Everyone always leaves me. It would be so good to have someone stay for a change."

The child was starved for attention, and so Sophie could forgive her this once. But such selfishness, and even unintended spite was something that Gertrude would need to temper before she made her debut. It concerned Sophie that the girl had been left so much alone, and that she had gotten so used to getting her own way that the happiness of others – if it might affect her – was not even a consideration.

The young woman needed her, and Sophie knew that she'd made the right choice to leave Alnerton and start again. Charlotte's happiness was complete, but Gertrude's was now beginning, and Sophie could be a part of it. She could help mold this budding young woman into a refined lady. She could make a difference in her life.

She may not have children, but it didn't mean she couldn't nurture Gertrude as if she were her own child. Sophie could be the mother figure that Gertrude lacked, due to the continuing physical absence of her own mother. She could be the positive influence that Gertrude needed to make her mark in the world. She hugged the young woman back. "Nor I, Gertrude. Nor I."

~

CLAVESTON DECIDED TO THROW A PARTY. It was quite the very best way to welcome Sophie to Compton Hall. Not only would it show her the high regard in which he held her but would also introduce her to Society – at least those in the county at present. He hurriedly sent out invitations to everyone in the county. He entrusted the task to Watkins, one of the stable lads. He was a swift rider and could be trusted not to dally. Many of his friends sent their acceptance back with the lad, who arrived back at Compton just before dinner - both he and his mount utterly exhausted. Claveston rewarded him with a couple of coins and ruffled the boy's unruly hair.

He was so excited about his plan, that he could barely contain himself over dinner that night – and though he usually requested his sister and Miss Lefebvre remain at the dining table whilst he enjoyed his cigars and port, he chose to retire to the library alone – in order to stop himself from blurting out the surprise.

He swore the staff to secrecy, and warned them all not to tell Gertrude, as she would never have been able to keep the news to herself – and would wish to come herself, which was out of the question. Claveston was not going to spend precious time he could be organizing his soiree on Gertrude's demands. She had a rather uncanny way of persuading him, just by wearing him down.

On the day of the party, he stopped by the kitchens. Cook was preparing a buffet of delicious treats, including many of Miss Lefebvre's favorites. She slapped his hands away as he tried to sample a little of everything and shooed him out of her domain. Mrs. Grint and the house-maids cleaned the house until it shone, and somehow, the secret had been kept, right up until the moment his guests began to arrive.

Claveston left Mrs. Grint expertly shepherding guests into a part of the house well away from where Miss Lefebvre and Gertrude were currently occupying themselves – which was also, thankfully, well away from the grand driveway that led from the road to Compton. Yet, he had still not told Miss Lefebvre. He paced up and down in his favorite drawing-room, wondering how to do so.

A soft tap on the door alerted him to Mrs. Grint's presence in the doorway. He looked up. "My Lord," Mrs. Grint informed him, with a slight frown. "Lady Alice Whyndam has arrived, with Lord Alfred Marchum."

He gave her a nervous grin. "Capital."

"I've shown them into the library, where Lord Henry Findlay and Miss Grace Ripperton are enjoying Cook's particularly spectacular seed cake."

"Good, good," Claveston said, rubbing his hands, delighted that his subterfuge was working, though also a little disconcerted by the look of disapproval on his housekeeper's face.

"My Lord, will other guests be joining us this evening?" the housekeeper asked, her tone respectful.

"Indeed, I expect a few more to arrive soon."

Mrs. Grint pursed her thin lips. "I see. And is Miss Lefebvre aware of this soiree?"

"Not yet," Claveston admitted. "As you know, it was planned as sort of a surprise for her."

"How considerate of you."

"I'm glad you noticed."

The older woman sighed. "My Lord, I do suggest you inform Miss Lefebvre of this evening's entertainments. I think you might find her otherwise disposed to a party. From what I have seen of Miss Lefebvre, she is not the kind of woman who is accustomed to such gatherings, at least not of the sort that those of your acquaintance prefer."

"What do you mean by that, Mrs. Grint?" Claveston asked, a little annoyed at her presumption. His friends were of the highest echelons of *the Ton*, the crème de la crème of county Society. There were future dukes and duchesses amongst his acquaintance, several earls, one or two barons, and even a few members of the merchant classes with great wealth and importance if not high birth.

What did Mrs. Grint know of Sophie? They'd only recently met. What woman didn't enjoy an evening of entertainment in her honor? "I am sure you are wrong, Mrs. Grint. She will enjoy the surprise and the opportunity to be better acquainted with our friends."

Mrs. Grint looked skeptical. "Perhaps. However, my observations of her say otherwise. She is not the kind of woman who enjoys the types of gatherings your friends do." Such candor was common for the doughty house-keeper. She always spoke her mind to everyone she met. It was a trait that both endeared and angered. But she was rarely wrong.

"My friends are the best of the Quality, Mrs. Grint,"

he said firmly. "I assure you that Miss Lefebvre is worthy of such society."

Mrs. Grint sighed. "Whether they are deserving of her is what I question," she remarked, before turning from the room, leaving Claveston speechless.

He went to storm after her but then paused. He could only hope that he was right and Mrs. Grint, for once, was wrong. It was too late to change his plans now. His friends were starting to gather, and that meant the party would go ahead whether Miss Lefebvre attended or not. It also meant that Gertrude needed to be in bed. She was too young for such an event. He took a deep breath and made his way along the corridors to the music room.

The sound of the pianoforte carried clearly throughout the east wing of the house. Claveston stopped outside the door for a moment, just listening. The tune was not the kind of cheery and uplifting music that Gertrude normally played. It was melancholic, haunting, and yet captivating at the same time. He leaned against the door, entranced by what he heard.

He remained transfixed until the music reached its final notes. Gathering himself, he pressed down on the handle and stepped inside. "Miss Lefebvre, Gertrude," he said, bowing to them both. He was taken aback for a moment, seeing his sister sat in the position he so often took for her, to turn the pages. It had been Miss Lefebvre playing. He shouldn't have been surprised. He knew well enough how accomplished she was, and yet he had not considered it might not be his sister playing.

Miss Lefebvre looked up and smiled. "Lord Wycliffe, can we 'elp you?"

"I'm sorry. I thought Gertrude was playing," he said a little foolishly.

"No," she replied. "It was me."

"Doesn't she play marvelously, Claveston? Sophie composed the piece herself."

"Miss Lefebvre, it seems you are all surprises," Claveston commented.

"How so?" She looked at him curiously.

"Who knew you could play so well? You never said anything."

"You never asked," Sophie remarked. She stood her hands folded demurely in front of her.

"I hope that such a reply means that I may ask about your other accomplishments in the future?" Claveston said with a flirtatious smile.

Miss Lefebvre blinked rapidly and looked a little awkward. Claveston wondered if he had, perhaps, been too forward. "You may ask whatever you like, my Lord," she said after a brief pause. "'owever, the right is mine whether I choose to answer."

He smiled. She was quite remarkable. "Very well said, Miss Lefebvre. I shall keep that in mind for the future."

He turned to his sister, whose eagle-eyes had narrowed a little at the exchange. He couldn't make out if she was amused or annoyed by it. But he did not have time to find out. "Time for bed, little sister," he said briskly. "Shall I see you to your room?"

Gertrude glanced at the grandfather clock and frowned. It was barely eight o'clock. "Why do you want me gone so early?" she asked, raising an eyebrow quizzically.

Claveston squirmed a little. "If I say it is your time for bed, then it is time for bed," he said trying his best to sound firm. "Don't argue with me." He grabbed his sister's arm and almost dragged her out into the corridor.

CHAPTER FIVE

"Do I hear your friends?" Gertrude asked as Lord Wycliffe escorted his sister to her rooms in the West Wing. Sophie followed on behind the fast-moving siblings, puzzled by the change in his behavior this evening. Lord Wycliffe looked more than a little uncomfortable and kept fidgeting with his cravat, something Sophie had noticed he did often when he had planned something he feared might not go down well with others.

"You do," he said a little irritably. "I have invited a few people so they might meet Miss Lefebvre." He didn't meet Gertrude's eye, or Sophie's. He stared ahead straight ahead, intent upon reaching his sister's suite. If he had looked back, he might have realized that Sophie wasn't much impressed by his obviously well-intended gesture for her. She was tired and longed for the peace and quiet of her rooms, so she might read for a time.

"Might I attend, too?" Gertrude begged, looking at her brother with wide, hopeful eyes. "I could perhaps practice all dear Sophie has been teaching me." Sophie was glad she was not the one to make such decisions for her – it would be very difficult indeed to say no to such a plea.

"Not tonight, Gertrude," Lord Wycliffe said firmly. "I don't think you are quite ready, yet."

"But I am," Gertrude protested as they reached her rooms. She opened the door and flounced towards her bed before sinking down on it. "And I have the most perfect party dress and have not had a single chance to wear it since the dressmaker delivered it weeks ago."

"No," Lord Wycliffe said firmly. "Now, to bed with you." He pressed a kiss to his sister's forehead and left the room, shutting the door firmly behind her.

"She will never truly learn how to behave in Society, if she is not in Society, my Lord," Sophie marked wryly. "She would comport herself well, I think."

"Not tonight," Lord Wycliffe said with a frown. "Tonight's entertainment is for you. If Gertrude attends, she will make it all about her – and I want you to have some fun for a change. You have been cooped up with Gertrude ever since you arrived. Don't you wish to meet some of my friends?"

There was no way to answer such a question politely. Sophie had little desire to make the acquaintance of his Lordship's friends. She could only assume that most of them would be like him – especially after the tales she had heard from William and Mary of the sorts of people they had encountered at one of his affairs in London.

"I should be delighted," she said politely. "But I must

wash and dress. I am not presentable to guests. I shall be down shortly."

"Thank you, Miss Lefebvre. You shall have a wonderful time, I promise you."

It did not take Sophie long to get ready, but she sat on her bed and waited for half an hour before she went downstairs. She needed to prepare herself. She did not like crowded affairs, a small card party or an intimate dinner with friends was much more her idea of a pleasant way to spend an evening. The noise level downstairs was rising, and she feared that the evening would be the worst kind of torment.

Yet Lord Wycliff had arranged the evening in her honor. In his confused way, he believed he was doing something good. Straightening her spine, holding her chin high, she took a deep breath and made her way downstairs to the drawing-room, where Lord Wycliffe and his friends were all gossiping and laughing amongst themselves.

Nobody even noticed her arrival. She wandered amongst them, catching snippets of conversation here and there. Much of the talk was about silly, trivial things she had no interest in – clothes, balls and possible matches. Not one person turned to greet her. She felt as invisible as the maids that provided an endless supply of drinks and tidbits. So much for the evening being arranged for her benefit.

Yet, it was fascinating being almost invisible to these people. One conversation made her stop and listen more closely. The talk in this little clique of women seemed to be of matches that they thought inappropriate. Sophie was aghast to hear names she knew all too well.

"The Duchy of Cott has little to be proud of," one rather spiteful woman said with glee. She was dressed in the finest burgundy silk, but her long face and straight, prominent nose made her rather resemble a horse. "First Lady Charlotte and that soldier of hers, son of a solicitor I believe."

"And then Lord William himself," her companion added breathlessly, her plump face and short stature a complete contrast to that of her tall, thin friend. "To that merchant's daughter. What was her name again, Honoria?"

"Mary Durand," the horsey lady said with a sneer. "And it isn't as if her dear Papa is even a real merchant, simply an inventor that got lucky. I'd wager the man's still got dirt under his fingernails."

Sophie glanced away from the pair, disgusted. She was surprised to see that Lord Wycliffe wasn't standing more than a few feet away. He must have heard what was being said – yet he had said nothing to defend his friends. Sophie shook her head. What kind of a man was he? Sophie scrutinized his face, trying to understand, but he seemed no more inclined to say anything, and so Sophie realized that she must.

"I can assure you that the new Lady Cott would never speak ill of a friend of this household," Sophie said pointedly, her voice loud and clear. Everyone turned to stare at her. She didn't care. Lord Wycliffe might permit his friends to be insulted in his presence, but Sophie would not. "She knows how to behave in company, and as for Capitaine Watts, he is more of a gentleman than any in this room will ever hope to be."

Lord Wycliffe looked ashamed, at least, but he didn't speak to support her, or William and Charlotte. When he finally did clear his voice, with a polite cough, he simply introduced her to the entire room. Sophie walked away from him, intent upon leaving the room and retiring to her rooms. She knew that Lord Wycliffe was vain and self-absorbed, but she had not taken him for a coward as well.

A tall and well-dressed gentleman stopped her just before she reached the door. "Everton Cormick," he said with a polite bow. "I just wanted to tell you I was very impressed with what you said. I attended school with Captain Watts and Lord Cott. They are both fine men, and I remember Cott's sister with great fondness. I recall she was rather formidable and knew her mind. I am not acquainted with Lady Mary, but I am told that she has a sweet disposition."

"They are amongst the finest people I know. I am honored to call them my friends," Sophie said, glad that at least one person here tonight seemed to hold the same opinion of the people she loved. Mr. Cormick was handsome, with sandy blonde hair that flopped in his bright blue eyes. He didn't seem affected in any way, his posture was upright, but not overly so. He was dressed well but was no dandy.

"Not many people would stand up to Lady Honoria that way," Mr. Cormick said admiringly.

"I see you didn't," Sophie said drily.

"Touché," Mr. Cormick said with an appealing grin. "You are right, and I must apologize for my tardiness in coming to your aid. I would make a terrible gallant knight, but to tell the truth, as I saw it, you did not need rescuing."

Sophie couldn't help but laugh at that. "You flatter me," she said, warming to the young man. "I was terribly rude."

"No, they were rude," Mr. Cormick insisted. "But they are always rude. They think that their wealth and position means that they have a right to be so. Yet, neither has yet found a husband who will put up with their shrewish ways and spiteful tongues – so perhaps they needed to be told."

"Thank you," Sophie said. "Now, I think I will retire. I am not made for such gatherings as this."

"I am sad to see you go," Mr. Cormick said, taking her hand and pressing a kiss to the back of it as he bowed. "If I might ever be at your service in any way, do not hesitate to let me know."

Sophie shook her head and smiled warmly at him. It was genuinely lovely to see a friendly face amongst the sea of eyes, all judging her without knowing a single thing about her. She curtseyed and made her escape.

~

CLAVESTON GLANCED around the room anxiously. Everyone seemed to have returned to their usual hum of gossip and nonsense, but Miss Lefebvre was nowhere to be seen. He knew he should have spoken up for William, and Charlotte – but he had never been one for making enemies. He hated confrontation and much preferred to ignore difficult matters than face them head-on. He had been shamed by what Miss Lefebvre had said, not because he disagreed with her – but because she had made him see what a coward he was, to not stand up for those he cared about.

Eventually, he found her. Mis Lefebvre was smiling and laughing with Everton Cormick, by the door. Whatever Cormick had said to her, he had clearly impressed her more than Claveston had ever managed to. She looked so happy, so beautiful and it made him peculiarly angry that it was Cormick who had brought her such joy and not himself. He was not entirely happy to realize that this was what jealousy felt like. He'd never felt it before – and there had never been anyone he had wanted to impress that much before.

He started to move towards them, then paused as he saw Cormick kiss Miss Lefebvre's hand before she curtseyed to him and left the room. Claveston was furious. She couldn't leave so early. The entire night was supposed to be for her. He had arranged everything, to please her. Her leaving meant he had failed, and he could not bear that thought.

Yet, he couldn't entirely blame her for wanting to go. Both he and his friends had behaved abominably. He had not done anything to protect her or to stand up for his absent friends. He hated the thought that, in her eyes, he was the lowest kind of worm. He hurried out of the room after her and chased up the stairs, catching her arm on the landing, as she went to take the second flight up. "Miss Lefebvre, please don't leave so early."

"Lord Wycliffe, this is not the place for such as me," she said firmly, turning to face him, her green eyes flashing with unspoken anger. "I am your sister's companion, and that is all. I am not your friend. Such an event for such as me is not appropriate."

"But I want you to be my friend," he said, aggrieved at her dismissal. He sounded like a petulant boy and as soon as he had uttered the words, he wished he could take them back.

"Then you should defend the friends you already 'ave," she said simply. "Would you 'ave stopped their gossiping if I had not done so?" She waited for a moment for him to answer, but she knew the answer without him saying a word. She turned away and continued to mount the stairs to her chambers. "And do you not think that they would 'ave been 'aving such a conversation at all, if the reason for their presence was not also inappropriate?" She paused for a moment and looked back at him, tears in her eyes. "Do you not see, that by throwing a party for me, to introduce me to them, that it makes them think I have ideas above my station?" She turned and ran up the rest of the stairs and disappeared.

Claveston hung his head. She was right. He hadn't thought any of it through, he couldn't argue that. He should have spoken for William, for James, for Charlotte and for Mary. They were not here to defend themselves. It had been his place to do so – and he had left it to Miss Lefebvre to speak on their behalf. He had arranged a party in Miss Lefebvre's honor, but not considered that doing so might in any way impugn her. Who threw a party for their sister's companion? It was not right – and he had made a fool of her, and of himself. Everyone downstairs must think him besotted, about to make a match as inappropriate as they thought William's and Charlotte's to be. Or, worse, they might think that Miss Lefebvre wished to rise in Society and was using him to do so.

He did not follow her. There was little point in trying to explain himself, for there were no excuses for his conduct. He was ashamed, and it was even more painful that she had seen right through him – that she knew that he was weak and nothing more than a dandy, following fashion, desperate to be accepted.

He ran back down the stairs and whispered to one of the footmen, then burst into the drawing room. "Party's over," he declared. "Your carriages are being brought round."

Everyone stared at him, as if he might be making some terrible joke, and they were waiting for him to reach the funny part. "I mean it," he said. "Please, just go. All of you."

They started to file out in twos and threes, muttering about what had come over him, and speculating that it must be to do with Miss Lefebvre's influence over him. Lady Honoria was not so discrete, confirming everything Miss Lefebvre had thrown in his face. "Are you the next among our circle to be considering marrying beneath your status?" she asked as she passed him by. "Your father would never permit it, you know. He'd never let his heir marry such an old maid. And one of the help? Lord Wycliffe, I thought more highly of you."

Claveston tried to bite his tongue. Lady Honoria was the daughter of one of his father's oldest and dearest friends. But her spite was quite repugnant. "Lady Honoria, if you wouldn't mind keeping your views to yourself, at least until you are no longer on my property, I would be most grateful," he said as politely as he could muster as he kissed her hand and bowed gallantly. She looked utterly put out at being spoken to that way, but she didn't utter another word until she left the house. Claveston saw that as at least a small victory.

Once all of his guests had departed, he sank down onto his favorite sofa and sighed heavily. Mrs. Grint entered the room and surveyed the debris his guests had left. "Things seem to have ended earlier than I might have expected," she said softly.

"You were right," Claveston admitted. "This was not the best idea I have ever had. Miss Lefebvre did not enjoy herself. My acquaintances, it turns out, are all spiteful and unpleasant jackals, out to rip everyone they think beneath them in any way to shreds."

"So, will we be expecting them again?" Mrs. Grint asked, her tone neutral, though Claveston was sure he could detect a hint of amusement in her grey eyes.

"I doubt it, Mrs. Grint. I doubt it," he said wearily.

"And, Miss Lefebvre," Mrs. Grint queried. "Is she alright?"

"Miss Lefebvre has the heart of a lion," Claveston said admiringly. "But I am sure that a pot of hot chocolate and a slice or two of cake would not go amiss if you were to take them up to her."

"I shall see to it right away," the housekeeper said and disappeared.

A flurry of housemaids appeared a few minutes later, cleaning around Claveston as he sat feeling sorry for himself. If he had thought to make a favorable impression tonight, he could not have failed more spectacularly.

CHAPTER SIX

The sun shone brightly when Sophie awoke the next day. She smiled sadly at the remains of the tray that Mrs. Grint had brought her, supposedly at Lord Wycliffe's request. It was the sort of gesture a man like him might make, rather than apologizing to her face, but it was at least something. She dressed and hurried downstairs to breakfast with Gertrude. Bonnet stopped her in the hallway and handed her a package.

"Oh, dear Sophie," Gertrude said excitedly as Sophie entered the breakfast room. "How was the party? You must tell me everything? I cannot wait until I am old enough to attend such events."

"It was just a party," Sophie said, setting down her package and opening it carefully. She smiled when she saw what was inside. "But I think you will be much more excited by what is in here."

"I will? What is it?"

"It is the sheet music we ordered," Sophie said,

pulling out the pages of music and passing them one at a time to Gertrude.

"Oh, how wonderful," Gertrude said, beaming as she traced her slender fingers along the lines of tiny black notes. "Will you teach me them this morning, the weather is due to remain fine all day. We could perhaps take our walk this afternoon, instead?"

"I do not see why not," Sophie said, as she helped herself to some food from the buffet and began to eat.

After they had eaten their fill, the pair went arm-in-arm to the music room and sat down at the pianoforte. Gertrude picked up the new tunes without much trouble and Sophie picked out the chords and improvised a second part, so they might perform them as duets. They laughed with each discordant choice Sophie made and paused until she had found something that worked better.

The morning flew by and Sophie was glad to have something so engrossing to take her mind from the events of the night before, but just before midday, Lord Wycliffe peered around the door, looking extremely sheepish. "Excuse me, might I have a quick word with you, Miss Lefebvre?" he asked tentatively. It was clear he hoped to be forgiven, though Sophie was disinclined to let him off without a real apology.

"We are in the middle of a lesson," she said firmly. "I will speak with you later."

Gertrude stared at her, then at her brother, who meekly disappeared and closed the door behind him. "Whatever is the matter? Has something happened between you two?" she asked.

"It is nothing," Sophie said hurriedly. Gertrude could be all too observant when she wished, and Sophie had no intention of saying anything bad about Lord Wycliffe to his doting sister, or risk having Gertrude taking his side over a matter that would be easily settled later on.

The rest of the lesson continued without incident, and Sophie sent Gertrude upstairs to wash before lunch, while she sought out Claveston. She found him in his favorite drawing-room, pacing up and down in front of the fireplace. "You wished to speak with me," she said, her tone icy.

"I did," he said, turning to face her. He wrung his hands nervously and fidgeted with his jacket and his waistcoat. "I wanted to say I am terribly sorry for what happened last night, that you were quite right. I should have said something. Lady Honoria was casting aspersions upon the character of the people I hold most dear to me, and I should have stopped her immediately. And I should have thought more upon how arranging such an event for you might appear. I never meant to harm you in any way. I truly thought it would be something nice for you."

Sophie shrugged. He was saying the right things, but she wasn't sure if he truly meant them. "I should not 'ave to tell you such things," she reminded him. "It is the kind of lesson I might need to teach someone of Gertrude's age, but you are a grown man. You should know better."

"You are right, absolutely right," Lord Wycliffe agreed nervously. "I am just not used to doing so. I have ever hated arguments, and it is easier to just let things pass me by – but I can promise you that this will be the last time it ever happens. I shall be a better friend, to you – and to William and Mary, James and Charlotte."

"Words are easy, Lord Wycliffe. It is by our actions we must be judged. But I believe that you mean what you say."

"I truly am so very sorry. I just wanted you to have a wonderful evening, to meet some people so you might feel you have friends nearby," he said with a wry chuckle. "I should have asked you first if such a thing would even be welcome?"

"Perhaps. It was a kind gesture. You simply got the execution a little wrong, and it meant that people were able to speculate and make it into something ugly," Sophie said generously. Poor Lord Wycliffe. He simply wasn't used to having to take responsibility for his actions – and how they might be perceived by others. His position in Society protected him. He could do whatever he liked. Nobody would ever say anything unpleasant to his face – though they might talk about him behind his back. But woe betide someone like Sophie setting her cap at a duke's son.

"Perhaps we might go on a picnic one day, the three of us?" she suggested, offering him something to prove she would not continue to hold it against him.

"I should like that," Lord Wycliffe said, his entire face lighting up in his delight at being forgiven. "Why not today? The weather is so fine, and I can ask Cook to pack up our lunch. We could take a walk through the woods, out towards the river?"

"Why not?" Sophie said, with a quiet chuckle herself. He was so easy to please, like a puppy dog.

As he hurried away, Sophie couldn't help reflecting that many of the concerns that Gertrude had might also apply to her brother. Just because he was older now did not mean that he had not been affected by the absences of his parents when he was her age. To be raised by nannies, housekeepers and servants was quite normal amongst the aristocracy, but most children knew that their parents were nearby. Lord Wycliffe and Gertrude had often not even known what country their parents might be in, and the constant concern over whether they might ever return from their long sea voyages must have left its mark upon both children.

Lord Wycliffe had perhaps enjoyed a little more stability once he had gone to school, but there would have been long periods without word from his family due to the vagaries of travel by ship. To watch his friends as they received letters from home, and for there to be nothing for him, must have been hard. And then to be showered with gifts and given all they could ever possibly imagine when their parents did finally return had left both of them with a sense of entitlement, that if they asked, they would receive.

Sophie had willingly offered her understanding to Gertrude. She was not responsible for the way she had been raised. Why did she expect more from Lord Wycliffe who had been raised the same way? He was a wealthy man, from an aristocratic line that could trace itself back to William the Conqueror. To do as one wished was what such men were used to doing. She had been spoiled, herself, from knowing Lord William and Captain Watts, who were both such good men, generous and kind. Perhaps she had forgotten that they were the exception and not the rule?

∼

DELIGHTED that Miss Lefebvre had given him a way to make things up to her, and to spend time with her, Claveston hurried to the kitchens and demanded that Cook change her plans for lunch, with just moments before service. She grumbled and frowned at him, but when he planted a kiss on her plump cheek, the old woman grinned and flicked a dishcloth at him. "Get away from me, you young devil," she said. "Don't think that you can charm me when you come into my kitchen with your demands – especially after all my hard work went to waste last night."

"It is not for me, Cook," Claveston assured her, "but for Miss Lefebvre and Gertrude. They have been cooped up in the music room all morning and are in need of some fresh air and delicious food – preferably combined in the form of one of your finest picnics."

"Get on with you," Cook said with a harrumph. "I'll send up some baskets in ten minutes."

Claveston beamed and grabbed an apple from the bowl on the sideboard. He took a big bite and made his way back upstairs. Miss Lefebvre was waiting in the hallway. Gertrude bounded down the stairs. Miss Lefebvre frowned. Gertrude immediately walked more sedately, her spine erect, her hand resting lightly upon the banister. Claveston couldn't help admiring the difference. His hoyden of a little sister was no more, in her place was a poised young lady.

"Congratulations," he said to Miss Lefebvre as Gertrude crossed the hallway, maintaining her poise. "I never thought I would live to see the day."

Miss Lefebvre giggled. Gertrude frowned as she approached them. "What is so funny," she asked petulantly. "Did I do it wrong?"

"Not at all," Miss Lefebvre assured her, putting an arm around Gertrude's waist and giving her an affectionate squeeze. "Quite the opposite. You were the perfect young lady. I was very proud."

"Me too," Claveston said, bending down to give her a peck on the cheek. Gertrude glowed under their praise, but Claveston also noticed that as soon as Miss Lefebvre turned away that Gertrude's smile faltered, replaced by a suspicious look for the fleetest of moments.

One of the kitchen maids appeared a few moments later, with a basket over each arm. Claveston took them, and the trio headed out into the sunshine. They walked through the formal gardens, Gertrude chattering on about the new pieces of music that she and Miss Lefebvre had been learning that morning, and how she had to walk for half an hour every day, up and down the long gallery, with books on her head to learn about comportment.

Claveston listened happily enough, glad that his sister seemed so happy. But what he really wanted was to learn more about Miss Lefebvre. He tried to ask her a few questions, but Gertrude always cut him off, with something else that Miss Lefebvre had taught her. He began to get a little impatient. He loved Gertrude dearly, but it was impolite of her to cut him off in such a manner and to almost totally exclude Miss Lefebvre from their conversation.

"Miss Lefebvre, what was it that brought you to England?" he asked when Gertrude briefly skipped on ahead of them.

"My father brought me when he came here to trade in England. I loved it very much."

"Come here, look," Gertrude called, beckoning them forward. "There are snakes here, two of them."

"I did not know there were snakes in England," Miss Lefebvre said with a shudder.

"We are blessed to only have those whose bite do no harm," Claveston said with a smile. "Adders and grass snakes only."

He hurried to catch up with his sister, but there was no sign of the snakes by the time he arrived. Gertrude tucked her arm through his. "They were there," she said, perhaps a little too vehemently. "Perhaps there will be otters in the river, today. I do so love the way they play together."

"If we are very still and very quiet," Claveston warned her. "You know they will not come if you are making lots of noise."

"I know," Gertrude said in a sing-song voice. "Run with me?"

"Young ladies do not run," he said, trying to be stern, but it was always hard when she grinned at him and hoicked up her skirts and scampered off expecting him to follow.

"She has enough time to be a young lady," Miss

Lefebvre said holding out her hands for the picnic baskets. "Let her enjoy being a child while she still can."

Claveston grinned, handed over the food, and raced after his sister, who squealed with delight when he caught her as they emerged from the woods near the riverbank and picked her up and spun her around. "I shall not be able to do this for much longer," he said sadly as he set her down and they picked a spot where they could lay out their blanket and enjoy their lunch.

As the siblings romped a little, Miss Lefebvre laid out the picnic. Gertrude flopped down onto the blanket. "I'm fashed," she said as she reached for a sandwich.

"You are fatigued," Miss Lefebvre corrected her. "A polite young woman never uses such vulgar words."

Gertrude sulked. She did not like being chastised. Claveston poured her a glass of lemonade and gave her a clandestine wink. She grinned back; she could never stay too mad when he was around. He was glad that it was so easy to appease her. Her mood seemed to be even more mercurial than usual, today.

"So, how are you settling in, Miss Lefebvre? I know I did not perhaps choose the right manner in which to introduce you to the local community, but what would be the right one?" he asked.

After thinking for a moment, Miss Lefebvre smiled. "We used to attend church in the village, and often undertook charitable work there."

"We can go to church this Sunday in Compton if you would like? We can call for the carriage – or perhaps even walk? I could show you some of the sights, hereabouts"

Claveston said, delighted that there might be something he could do for her.

Gertrude rolled her eyes as Miss Lefebvre nodded. "That would be lovely," she said. "Thank you."

"Are we quite done?" Gertrude demanded rudely as she set down her plate and stood up to go.

Claveston was mortified. Miss Lefebvre had barely taken a morsel of food, she had been too busy ensuring that he and Gertrude were served first. Gertrude was acting as though she were a child, and not the young woman he had hoped she was becoming under Miss Lefebvre's tutelage. He simply did not know what had gotten into her.

"We should give your companion a moment to eat, at least, do you not think?" he reminded his sister, who stomped away from them and stared out over the river.

Claveston looked at Miss Lefebvre who could not even meet his eye. "I am sorry," she muttered.

"Such behavior is hardly your fault," Claveston assured her. "I shall speak with Gertrude when we get home. She knows better than to be so rude."

"It is my duty to prepare her for polite Society, that she is not yet there reflects badly upon my teaching."

"No, it does not," Claveston assured her. "You have been here a very short time. I have been responsible for Gertrude, and it is my fault that she is so spoiled."

Miss Lefebvre raised a quizzical eyebrow. "Not your parents' responsibility?" she asked. "You are just her brother. You are not her guardian, or her tutor."

"I suppose you are right. But I have been the only permanent presence in her life. If she is ill-mannered, it is because I have let her be that way. I hate to scold her, and she knows it."

"Yes," Miss Lefebvre said with a smile. "I 'ave noticed that neither of you takes well to being told what to do."

Claveston laughed out loud, causing Gertrude to turn and glare at them both. "But I am at least trying to learn how to change," he assured her.

"I suppose you are," she said graciously. "Perhaps we should go back to the house now, before poor Gertrude explodes from her frustrations?"

They packed up the remains of the picnic and called to Gertrude who dawdled behind them on the way back through the woods. They were about to cross through the gate into the formal gardens when they heard a loud cry of pain from somewhere behind them.

Claveston turned and ran back. He found Gertrude lying on the ground, writhing in agony, clutching at her left ankle. "I must have twisted it," she said between moans. "I am so clumsy, I wasn't looking where I was going, must have trodden in a rabbit hole or something, and lost my balance. Before I knew it, here I was."

Feeling worried, Claveston picked Gertrude up and carried her into the house, Miss Lefebvre hurrying at his side, her face a picture of concern. He laid Gertrude down on the chaise in the library, while Miss Lefebvre fetched bandages, hot water and sent one of the maids to the icehouse so she could make a cold compress for Gertrude's ankle.

While she was gone, Claveston inspected Gertrude's supposedly twisted ankle. There were no signs of swelling or redness, not even a scratch from the branches that littered the ground in the woods. He looked into his sister's face, hoping that the little minx hadn't manufactured this entire scenario in order that she might be the center of attention once more. But even Gertrude was not so spoiled, was she?

CHAPTER SEVEN

A number of days had passed since the picnic. Gertrude hobbled around when she thought she was being watched, but Sophie was sure that she saw her walking and running without trouble on a number of occasions. She did not say anything. It seemed clear enough that the girl was struggling with something and acting out. The last thing she needed was more attention, to reinforce the bad behavior.

"How is your poor ankle today?" she asked her young charge over breakfast. "We 'ave not practiced your dancing or your comportment for some days now, and they are not skills that any young lady should be without."

"It feels a little better," Gertrude said piously. "I think I could manage something, as long as it is not too sprightly."

"We can learn the Pavane," Sophie said patiently. "It is quite simple and sedate. It shouldn't tax your poor ankle too greatly."

But before they had even finished eating, the sound of the front doors of the hall bursting wide open and a slightly accented female voice called out loudly "Where are you all?"

Gertrude beamed from ear to ear and burst from the breakfast room, forgetting completely to limp at all. "Mama," she cried.

By the time Sophie had emerged from the breakfast room, her young charge was being held tightly and smothered with kisses by an elegantly dressed, very regal looking lady. "There are a hundred gifts for you, my darling, in my trunks. Why don't you go and hurry Bonnet along, so you can fetch them and tell me what you think?" she said, caressing Gertrude's face and then ushering her outside.

"*Et vous, je présume que vous êtes Mademoiselle Sophie Lefebvre,*" she said, her French perfect.

"*Oui, Lady Compton,*" Sophie replied bobbing a curtsey.

"*Je suis ravi de vous rencontrer,*" Lady Compton went on, as she took off her gloves and hat and handed them to a nearby maid. "*Claveston m'a parlé des merveilles que vous accomplissez avec la chère Gertrude. Elle est un peu indisciplinés, mais si cher, ne pensez-vous pas?*"

"I would 'ave to agree," Sophie said with a smile. "But you need not speak French on my account, though I must compliment you on your grasp of my country's language."

"Nonsense, you need not compliment me at all," Lady Compton said with a grin, her English accent as clean and crisp as Charlotte's, as she tucked her arm through Sophie's and began to lead her to the drawing-room. "I myself am also French. It is a pleasure to have someone else to talk to in the most beautiful language there is."

She sat down on an armchair by the window. "And where is my son?" she asked looking around.

"I'm here, Mama," Claveston said bounding into the room and pressing a kiss to his mother's powdered cheek. "How was your trip? Did you find the perfect armoire you set out to find?"

"You know, I did not," Lady Compton admitted. "But I did find an escritoire which will be perfect for those empty rooms in the West Wing."

"They are no longer empty, Mother," Claveston said grinning as he sat down opposite her on the sofa. "I arranged for them to be opened for Miss Lefebvre."

"But they are unfinished?" Lady Compton said aghast. "I have new wall hangings and carpets, and so much furniture for them."

"They are quite perfect as they are," Sophie assured her, smiling. "I do not think I 'ave ever had such perfectly appointed rooms."

"Pish," Lady Compton said with a wave of her hand. "We shall have you moved into the Queen's suite whilst I finish working my magic. Then you will see perfection."

"Thank you, Lady Compton," Sophie said, realizing that there was little point in arguing with this formidable woman.

As she took a seat by the window, Sophie couldn't help thinking that she had been prepared to dislike Gertrude and Lord Wycliffe's parents on sight, due to their callous disregard of their children. But it was impossible not to admire this remarkable woman. She was a force of nature, vivid and brilliant, strong and independent. Such a free spirit should not be tamed, and being a mother did not always suit every woman – no matter what men might think.

Gertrude entered the room carrying an armful of perfectly wrapped gifts, two of the household servants following on behind with an open trunk behind her. "Mama brought us so many things," she said excitedly.

"Including the fabrics we will need to have all your dresses made so you may have your Coming Out this year," Lady Compton said, getting up and handing Claveston a pile of parcels, and then a few to Sophie, too.

Sophie held them on her lap as she watched Claveston and Gertrude opening theirs. Their mother had brought everything she could think of that a young man and young woman might want – except her own presence. Sophie opened her own gifts and was stunned to find a diamond necklace with matching earrings, some ivory combs, and a bolt of cloth that she could have made into an evening gown. "This is too much," she protested. "I 'ave no need of such riches."

"Nonsense," Lady Compton said. "I cannot have you escorting my daughter around London dressed like a beggar."

"Mother," Claveston said with a grin, "I can assure you that Miss Lefebvre does not possess anything that might make her even vaguely resemble a beggar."

"Nonetheless, she will have an entirely new wardrobe. My seamstress will attend her, and Gertrude tomorrow. There is much to get ready, and not enough time."

Sophie glanced at Gertrude, who was still unwrapping gifts with the enthusiasm of a child. "Ahem," she said, clearing her throat a little. "I do not wish to speak out of turn, but I am not sure if Lady Gertrude is quite ready to 'ave her first Season."

Both Gertrude and her mother turned and glared at Sophie. "Then the two of you have much to do, do you not?" Lady Compton said peremptorily. "My daughter will be presented at court this year as she turns sixteen. Every girl in the St. John family has been presented at sixteen. I will not be the only mother not to manage that."

"Yes, my Lady," Sophie said, bobbing a curtsey. "Then we should perhaps continue with your lessons, Gertrude, don't you think?"

Gertrude frowned. She obviously did not wish to be taken away from her mother, or her gifts. But the promise of her first Season did much to dispel her unhappiness. She followed Sophie to the music room, where she applied herself wholeheartedly to her dance lessons and even agreed to practice more in her spare time.

~

THE MOOD in the house seemed lighter since Mama's arrival and that concerned Claveston. Mama could be charming, delightful and full of excitement when she was wrapped up in a project, and it seemed to him that getting Gertrude ready for a London Season could easily be put into that category. Yet, she could bore of her passions just as quickly as she took them up, and Claveston was not sure how Gertrude would deal with that, especially with so much at stake this time.

Claveston had seen a real change in Gertrude, and even in Miss Lefebvre since Mama had reappeared in all their lives. Both of the younger women seemed more relaxed, happier even. He often found Miss Lefebvre and Mama together, chattering in French as they picked out patterns, colors, and fabrics for Gertrude's gowns, and made plans for the kinds of events that she should attend once in London. He could see that Sophie was growing close to Mama, and he hated the thought that she might be hurt if Mama's affections were snatched away, as they so often were, without notice.

Yet despite his concerns, it was a delight to see them getting on so well, and he knew that his mother appreciated Miss Lefebvre's tendency to speak her mind, as she had done in the drawing-room on Mama's first day home when she had pointed out her concerns about whether Gertrude would be ready. It was such a French thing. Mama did it too. They simply didn't see that by being honest that they might be seen as being rude. It was as charming as it was infuriating.

However, Gertrude had not taken her companion's words as well as it might at first have seemed. Claveston had noticed the occasional flashes of anger that crossed his younger sister's features when Miss Lefebvre was not looking, though she had seemed keen to continue her lessons ready for her Season and was a diligent student in every way.

Yet, something nagged at Claveston. There had been

too many odd looks, and there was the bad ankle that had never shown any signs of damage that had so magically healed the day Mama returned home. It puzzled Claveston. Gertrude might be mercurial, but she was not usually so secretive, or so deceitful.

He was glad to note that he had noticed less of such moments since his mother's return, which was at least a blessing of sorts. Mama doted upon Gertrude, lavishing her with the attention his young sister craved so desperately. She blossomed under the attention – and that left Claveston full of fear as to what might happen when Mama undoubtedly disappeared again once her interest in being a parent dissipated. Mama could only be delightful and charming with children for so long, after all.

It also concerned him that Mama had talked only of Miss Lefebvre accompanying Gertrude through her Season - and hadn't once said whether or not she would be there to present her daughter at Court – let alone any of the balls and assemblies she had insisted were the places to be seen. A daughter needed her mother at such a time in her life. There was so much to navigate, and though he did not doubt that Miss Lefebvre was up to the task, it should not be hers to bear.

Knowing that there may be a gaping hole torn into their lives again, before any of them were ready for it, Claveston knew he needed to make sure that Gertrude knew she was loved. He decided that it was time to spend some time with his little sister so she might be better prepared for Mama's unknown but inevitable departure.

He'd barely seen Gertrude, except at dinner for

weeks, she had been so caught up in all the preparations and all of her lessons. He poked his head around the music room door, knowing that was where they could often be found after lunch, and grinned when he saw her with Miss Lefebvre, practicing a cotillion. Poor Gertrude kept moving forward when she should wait and was often tempted to dance the man's part rather than her own.

"Do you need rescuing?" he said with a grin.

Gertrude glanced over at him and rewarded him with a delightful smile. "Oh, would you?" she begged.

"Do you mind, Miss Lefebvre?" he asked her. "I feel I have barely seen my sister in weeks, whilst you ladies all plan and plot for the most perfect Coming Out there has ever been."

Miss Lefebvre smiled, too. Just seeing her so content brought Claveston such joy, even if it was tinged with concern. The atmosphere at Compton had truly changed in recent weeks, and he hoped that she was glad to have come to Compton. He knew he was glad that she was here. "Go," she assured her pupil. "We 'ave time for you to get this right. Perhaps we can convince your Mama to let us roll back the rugs in the drawing-room and practice after supper. I am sure that your brother would make a fine partner to help me show you 'ow these complex group dances work."

"I should be delighted to accompany you, Gertrude," Claveston said and was rewarded with another bright smile from his sister and her companion.

He offered Gertrude his arm and the two of them left. "What should you like to do?" he asked her.

"May we go riding?" Gertrude asked. "I've barely had

time to visit Moonlight since Mama returned, much less take her for a gallop."

"If you were a man, you'd be a neck-or-nothing rider, would you not?" Claveston teased.

"I should enjoy the chance," Gertrude admitted as they walked around the house to the stables. "Why are women not permitted to do anything that is truly enjoyable?"

"You are permitted to do all manner of things."

"But not to go to school or university, I am only permitted on the hunt here because nobody wishes to upset you or Papa, but heaven help me if I should wish to hunt anywhere else."

"It is just the way the world is," Claveston said with a sigh. He often wondered why women were held back from doing so many things that were deemed healthy and invigorating for men yet damaging to young women. It made little sense to him. Surely a healthy enjoyment of exercise and fresh air was good for anyone?

Claveston nodded to one of the stable lads who disappeared into the stalls and brought out his bay stallion, and Gertrude's grey mare. He had bought the feisty horse for Gertrude's fourteenth birthday. The two were quite a pair, and there were few riders in the county that would keep up with them.

Gertrude nuzzled Moonlight's neck and rubbed her nose lovingly. The horse nickered a greeting, as the stable lad went to fetch Gertrude's side-saddle. "Miss Lefebvre said that even if I can take Moonlight with me to London that I will not be permitted to do more than trot in the park."

"That would be terrible," Claveston said solemnly, as he threw his own saddle onto Hector's back, amused by his sister's serious face. "Perhaps I can come and take you out from time to time. There are places I know that are away from prying eyes where you might have a good gallop."

"Would you do that for me?" Gertrude asked, brightening immediately as she fitted Moonlight's bridle and bit herself, then used the stable-lad's proffered hands to boost herself up into the saddle. She arranged her skirts as she had been taught, and sat erect, her hands light on the reins.

It hurt that she was often so easily pleased. She did not really need all of the gifts and trinkets that Mama and Papa showered upon her. All she longed for was for them to notice her, to spend time with her. She was just a little girl who longed to be loved. "I shall be delighted to do just that," Claveston assured her, "and shall make sure I find time to do so at least once every single week that you are in London, come what may."

"You promise?"

"I promise. You will need the escape from all those tedious afternoon teas and dances. It might seem exciting now, but months and months of it would drive even the most eager young woman half mad." Gertrude giggled.

They rode out of the yard, the horses' hooves clip-clopping on the cobbles until they reached the grasslands where Gertrude urged Moonlight to a canter. Claveston did the same, but stayed just behind his sister, watching the way she handled Moonlight. She was one of the finest riders he'd ever seen, and he loved to watch the way she guided Moonlight with soft touches and light hands. He'd not ever seen her tug on Moonlight's tender mouth, or use a riding crop, so in tune with one another were horse and rider.

As they rode further out of sight of the house, Gertrude grinned and urged the gallop. She raced away. Hector was a fine, strong horse, but he struggled to match the pace of the faster mare. Gertrude flew, her hair streaming behind her, all worries thrown to the winds. Claveston whooped his appreciation for her form and was delighted to lose to her when she bet him that she would reach the river first.

As they let their mounts rest and take a well-earned drink, brother and sister sat down, side by side, on the riverbank. "Do you like Miss Lefebvre?" Gertrude asked him unexpectedly.

"Of course," he said awkwardly. "She is a fine young woman, and an excellent companion, don't you think?"

"I suppose so," Gertrude said. "I've not had one before, so cannot tell. But that isn't quite what I meant. There are times... times when I catch you looking at her." She looked at him intently. "Would you wish to marry her, Claveston, if you could?"

It was such a peculiar question, and one he wasn't entirely sure he wished to answer. If all things were possible, then he would certainly like to entertain such a possibility – but Miss Lefebvre was a member of their household now. It would be quite improper. But he did not want to lie to his sister and deny that he was most certainly fascinated by the unusually beguiling Frenchwoman.

He pursed his lips. "I am fond of Miss Lefebvre, it is true. She is quick-witted, accomplished, rather lovely to look at - and if we were compatible then I might perhaps consider a union, but..." he tailed off. He wasn't explaining it well, but it seemed that his sister had heard enough.

"If you were to marry, would you leave here?" she asked him. "I mean, to set up a home elsewhere?"

"Why would I do that?" Claveston asked, a little confused by the peculiar questions. "This is my home, and yours. The furthest I might go would be to the town-house in London – and you shall be there with me this year for the Season."

"All my nannies left when they married," Gertrude said sadly. "I should hate it if you went, too."

At times, especially since Miss Lefebvre had been at Compton and had been helping Gertrude, Claveston forgot how very young she still was. He put an arm around her shoulder and hugged her close. "I am not one of your nannies," he assured her. "If I marry," he paused, he did not wish to give her some kind of false hope that such a thing might not happen. "When I marry, Compton will still be my home. I am heir to the Duchy, and Papa relies upon me to run the place while he is gone. I will never leave."

Gertrude gave him a peculiar look. He wasn't sure if he had eased her mind or not. "If anything, Gertie, it will be you who leaves me when you find a rich duke to marry you." He kept his tone light and teasing, and Gertrude smiled, but he wasn't sure if he'd said the right thing to reassure her.

"Shall we go home," she said, moving towards her horse and taking the reins ready to mount. She was not happy, but Claveston did not know what she wanted him to say. He had been as truthful as he could be – and surely that was for the best?

With a heavy sigh, he offered her his cupped hands and threw her up into the saddle. He watched as she settled herself, wondering what had gotten into her, to have her seem so sad and serious. He would speak with Mis Lefebvre when they returned and ask if she might keep an extra eye on Gertrude. He didn't know precisely why, but he was worried about her.

CHAPTER EIGHT

As time passed, and the preparations for Gertrude's first Season began to bear fruit, Sophie realized that she had finally started to feel at home here at Compton. Having someone to talk to in French, and their shared goal to prepare Gertrude so she could face any eventuality gave her days real purpose. Evening dinners had become lively affairs, with Lady Compton holding forth upon her many adventures, and Lord Wycliffe teasing his mother and sister good-naturedly. Sophie was even coming to see a side to him that she hadn't seen before, the generous, loving, and devoted one that cared deeply about his family. She rather liked that Claveston St. John.

One afternoon, she bumped into Mrs. Grint on the stairs. The poor woman was trying to balance two heavily laden trays that she was bringing down from Lady Compton's suite. "Let me 'elp you," she offered taking one of them before the elderly housekeeper could say no.

"You do not need to," Mrs. Grint said, but grimaced a little as she took a few steps down.

"Is your knee troubling you, again?" Sophie asked. She knew that the older woman had a few niggles, especially when the weather turned cold and wet as it had done over the past few days.

"A little. The liniment you got for me from the village has been a great help."

"I am glad."

"You're doing a fine job, with Lady Gertrude," Mrs. Grint said, nodding her head sagely. She wasn't much given to praise, so Sophie treasured the comment.

"She is a good girl, though I fear she lacks discipline."

"Aye, they both struggle with that, her and Lord Claveston," Mrs. Grint agreed. "They're loving enough, but they've been both starved of affection and spoiled with everything their little hearts could ever desire. I don't think anyone's ever said no to either of them before you."

"I don't exactly say no to them," Sophie said.

"Oh, you do – in your way. You show Lady Gertrude how she should behave, rather than screaming and shouting – or pouting – until she gets what she wants, she is seeing that you are prepared to wait until you have earned it. Learning by example is a powerful thing."

"I agree," Sophie said. "I think shouting at Lady Gertrude or telling her what to do would 'ave the opposite effect to what I want from her."

"You're right enough about that." Mrs. Grint chuckled as they crossed the hall and into the back corridor. "It's a shame young Claveston never had anyone like you around when he was a boy. Maybe then he'd be more inclined to take a wife."

"You think he's avoiding it?" Sophie asked, curious as to the older woman's answer. It had often struck her as peculiar that Claveston seemed to show no interest in finding a bride. She knew all too well the pressure that a man like him must be under, from his parents and Society, to wed and produce an heir. Yet, she had never heard his name linked to that of any of the eligible young women of his acquaintance.

"I fear he is as troubled by the thought of people leaving him as dear Lady Gertrude is," Mrs. Grint said as they made their way down the back stairs to the kitchens. "I fear for him, that he may end up a bounder, even a cad."

"You do?" Sophie said, surprised at such a thing. She knew, from Charlotte and William, that Lord Wycliffe enjoyed his parties and that he had been known to gamble from time to time, but she had not heard anything from them about any affairs he might have enjoyed. They never spoke of him in that way.

"You know, I think that this may be the longest that her Grace has spent here at Compton, in one visit that is. His Grace is here even less. Those children grew up knowing that their parents could only love them in small bites. It isn't good for a child to be always alone with strangers who come and go as they have."

"It must 'ave been very hard on them."

"Aye, it was," Mrs. Grint agreed. "And I fear that

neither will ever trust anyone enough to let them love them. But they are such good souls, they deserved so much more."

Sophie pondered the older woman's words as she went back upstairs and into the small drawing-room. It wasn't as opulent as the one Lord Wycliffe favored, with its faded brocade chaises and light oak furnishings. It was a very feminine room, and Sophie found it a calming place to sit and think. It also housed a rather lovely old harpsichord, which she was teaching herself to play.

Whenever she was troubled, she had always found music to be a salve for her frayed nerves. And after her conversation with Mrs. Grint, she had much on her mind. Sophie sat down at the bench and let her fingers fly over the keys. They were much stiffer than those of the pianoforte and reacted to her touch more slowly, but she loved the sound that they drew, so bright and light – perfect to play the music of Mozart upon. She was soon lost in her favorite sonata, letting the melody soothe her as she added the changes in tempo, mood, and the dynamics of loud and soft it required to bring it to life.

She was so lost in her playing, that she didn't notice Lord Wycliffe leaning in the doorway, listening to her, his expression dreamy – as if lost somewhere far away. When she did, she stopped playing abruptly. He blinked a few times, as if coming out of a trance, and then smiled at her. "You have such a wonderful gift," he said admiringly, "to be able to play so beautifully."

"I do love to play," Sophie admitted as he moved into the room. "It is such an escape."

Somehow, though the room was amply sized, his presence made it seem somehow small and cramped. Sophie had not ever felt so aware of his presence before. She wondered if it was because they had never been alone before, there was always someone else present. He did not draw any nearer, but it still felt as if he was right beside her, his warmth filling the space between them as if he was sitting beside her on the stool.

He perched on the back of one of the chaises and extended his leg. She couldn't help noticing his shapely calves, though she forced herself to look away. He was dressed in a plain green velvet jacket today. It was unusually somber for him, he usually favored intricately embroidered waistcoats and bright colors. Seeing him this way it felt as if she was finally seeing the man hiding behind the dandy. It was disconcerting. Somehow their meeting this way seemed somehow untoward, clandestine, and Sophie felt a flush of heat suffuse her skin, from her chest to her cheeks.

"I often wish I had learned to play," Lord Wycliffe said sadly.

"But you 'ave a fine tenor voice," Sophie said nervously. She and Gertrude had often accompanied him as he sang for them after dinner. "I cannot sing a note. You cannot be blessed with every gift."

"Indeed, that would be quite greedy of me, would it not?" he said with a grin. "But I fear it may be the only one I possess."

"I doubt that, my Lord," Sophie said softly. "There are many things that you excel in I am sure."

They looked at one another awkwardly, neither

knowing what else to say. The atmosphere between them felt charged, as if they had crossed some kind of barrier that they had both been trying not to. Sophie fidgeted with the ringlets that hung down around her face nervously, as she tried to think of what to say next. Lord Wycliffe picked at a loose thread on the back of the chaise, his eyes never leaving her face, not even for a moment. Sophie felt he was looking right through her, though she had no idea what he thought he was seeing.

Finally, after what felt like an eternity had passed, Lord Wycliffe stood up. He smoothed the wrinkles in his jacket and turned to leave. He paused in the doorway and looked back at her. "My friend, Everton Cormick, is to join us for dinner this evening. I hope you do not mind. He wished to pay his respects to Mama before she decides to leave again. You seemed to at least not mind his company, when he was last here." There was an edge in his voice as if he expected her to object, or perhaps to be delighted by such news.

"He was kind to me," Sophie admitted cautiously, not sure why she felt that she should answer him so carefully. "I shall make sure that Gertrude is prepared for company. Perhaps we can convince the two of you to accompany us so she may practice her dancing?" She smiled tentatively, knowing that though Claveston often assisted her in teaching his sister to dance, it was not one of his favored pastimes.

"I am sure we shall bear it, as it is for such a fine cause," Claveston said, looking amused. "I shall see you at seven."

He left the room, leaving Sophie feeling confused

and disconcerted. There had, at times, been something almost flirtatious in their conversation, or so it had seemed to her. She had surely been imagining it, because Claveston St. John would not be flirting with a mere lady's companion like herself. His father would intend him for someone like Charlotte, the daughter of a duke or a marquess, or an earl at the very least. Yet at others, there had been an undercurrent of something much darker coming from Lord Wycliffe, and anger or jealousy perhaps, and she did not know why.

Before going upstairs, she ordered a bath to be sent up to her rooms. When the maids had finished filling it with steaming buckets of water, Sophie sank into the rose-perfumed water and wondered about everything that had happened with Lord Wycliffe. It did not make sense to her at all. The richly perfumed water began to work its magic though, and her mind eased leaving her free to daydream.

She closed her eyes and wondered what it might be like to be married to someone – anyone. But as she let her imagination run free the man beside her at the altar, and opposite her at the dining table was no longer faceless, as he had been throughout so much of her life. Now he possessed the face of Lord Wycliffe, and no matter how hard she tried to banish the image of his handsome face, Sophie couldn't seem to imagine it any other way. And he was a good husband. Loving, devoted, loyal – and happy to stay home with her and build a family.

It was a pretty picture indeed, but so far from what could ever happen in reality, that Sophie vowed to put it from her mind as soon as she got out of the tub. But as she dressed and fixed her hair, brief glimpses popped, unasked for, into her mind. She shook her head and hummed loudly as she made her way to Gertrude's chambers. At least she would have no time for such silly nonsense as she got the young woman ready for her first real test. Gertrude's chatter alone would keep her distracted enough, surely?

~

A LOUD BANGING upon the door announced Everton Cormick's arrival at the house. Claveston ran from the library into the hallway to greet his friend. He stopped abruptly when he saw Bonnet walking sedately, his back as straight as a poker and his hawklike nose in the air, towards the large oak doors. The butler opened them wide and stepped aside to let Cormick inside. Claveston stepped forward to greet his friend with a firm handshake, before Cormick removed his hat and coat and handed them to Bonnet.

"So, old man," Cormick said as Claveston guided him towards the library, where he had a fine claret awaiting. "How goes life in the country?"

"Well," Claveston said. "And how are matters in London?"

"Dull," Cormick said with a smile as they entered the library. "But I did not come here to talk business. How is Miss Lefebvre? I must confess to being quite taken with her. She is quite lovely." He sank into one of the comfortable armchairs by the fireplace.

Claveston frowned as he moved to the small table

where he had placed the decanter of wine and two glasses. In his pleasure at his friends' arrival, Claveston had briefly forgotten that Cormick was the only person that Miss Lefebvre had really spoken with intimately at his failed party and had just allowed himself to be happy to see the man. With Cormick's innocent comments, all of Claveston's jealousies reared to the fore once more. He hated that he was so possessive of Miss Lefebvre. Surely if he truly cared for her, he would want the very best for her? And there was no denying that Cormick was a better man than he would ever be.

"She is well," he said hastily answering Cormick's question as he poured a glass of the rich red liquid and handed it to his friend. "She will be joining us for dinner, along with my dear Mama and Gertrude."

"How delightful," Cormick said looking genuinely pleased. "I heard a rumor that Lady Gertrude is to make her debut this Season?"

"She is, and I would be grateful if you might ensure that she has at least one dance on her card filled if you are ever attending any of the same events, old friend."

"I should be delighted. She has always been a spirited little thing. She will make someone a fine wife someday."

"I doubt that," Claveston said with a chuckle as he poured himself a glass and took a sip. "The girl is a hellion."

"There are some men that would prefer that," Cormick said seriously. "I cannot imagine anything more unpleasant than an insipid Bath Miss."

"You'll not find any of those at our table," Claveston

said as he took a seat opposite his friend. "Mama is, as you know, a force of nature, Miss Lefebvre is most definitely a woman of spirit – and Gertrude, well, she is learning how to behave in polite Society, but she is impetuous and often forgets her manners."

"And you would not wish to change any of them," Cormick said chuckling.

"Sometimes I would," Claveston admitted. He would willingly temper his Mama's wilfulness with a small dose of motherly feeling if he could.

A gong sounded across the hallway. "Ah, dinner is ready," Cormick said jumping to his feet. "I am famished, old boy. I do hope that your wonderful Cook has made that delicious venison dish she made last time I was here."

"I believe we have beef," Claveston said a little distractedly as he saw Miss Lefebvre descending the stairs through the open doorway. As she disappeared out of sight, he shook his head almost imperceptibly, stood up, and slapped his friend affectionately on his back. "But I can assure you, it will be just as fine."

Mama was already seated at the head of the table when they arrived. Claveston should have been put out. In his father's absence, he was supposed to be the head of the household, but he would never gainsay his mother, and most certainly would not ever do so in public. She rose briefly so that Cormick might kiss the back of her hand and bow graciously to her, then sank back down and flicked open a feathered fan and wafted it in front of her face.

Miss Lefebvre and Gertrude were stood by their seats, both looked lovely, their hair pinned in concoctions of elaborate plaits and curls that framed their lovely faces. Claveston smiled at Miss Lefebvre as Gertrude dropped into a very elegant curtsey and held out her hand for Cormick to take. Cormick kissed the air above Gertrude's skin politely.

Miss Lefebvre smiled back at Claveston. Her pupil had learned a great deal in a very short time. She switched her attention back to Gertrude and nodded approvingly as Cormick gallantly offered Gertrude his arm and escorted her to her place at the table, while Claveston did the same for Miss Lefebvre. "She did that rather well, did she not?" he whispered as Gertrude took her seat and nodded politely to Cormick.

"Yes, she did," Miss Lefebvre said as she took her own seat and smiled encouragingly at Gertrude.

Mama had seated Cormick next to Miss Lefebvre, and so Claveston took the seat by his sister. He could have chosen to sit at the foot of the table, though the head was technically his right in his father's absence - but in a strange way that felt too much as though he truly was acceding all power to his mother. By choosing not to take her seat at the table, he would also be closer to everyone and they could all converse more easily. The last thing he wanted was for Cormick to be able to monopolize Miss Lefebvre all night.

Yet, as the meal progressed through the soup and fish courses, it was clear that Cormick and Miss Lefebvre were enjoying a number of private moments, despite his choice of seat. Claveston often caught the two of them laughing at something that he'd not heard, and he did not like being on the outside one bit. He had to choke down his jealousy on a number of occasions, and he didn't like himself for it. Cormick was a good man. The best of men. He would make a fine husband – certainly a better one than Claveston would. He knew how to give love and accept it freely. Miss Lefebvre deserved someone that could offer her that.

As he glanced around the table, it seemed that Gertrude wasn't too pleased about the way the evening was progressing either, as she began to forget the manners that Miss Lefebvre had been so diligently teaching her, and rather than waiting to be asked a question began to try and dominate the conversation with the things she had learned that day. Claveston wasn't sure if she wanted Miss Lefebvre's attention most, or Cormick's, but she seemed determined to get someone's.

"Mama," she said eagerly as they awaited the arrival of the roast beef. "You must come and see the watercolor I painted today. Miss Lefebvre says it is quite the best one I have ever done."

"I am sure that can be arranged," Mama said a little wearily, as if she was already growing bored with family life and the little things that a mother should be happy to give to their children – like encouragement and praise. Claveston was not surprised that the bored comment was soon followed with a rebuke. "Though a young lady should wait to be asked about her accomplishments, not simply blurt them out at the dinner table. And it is quite vain of you to remark upon how good they are yourself." He winced on Gertrude's behalf.

His sister frowned at the gentle scolding and glared briefly at her mother and then at Miss Lefebvre who was biting at her lip anxiously. Claveston caught the gentle nod of encouragement from teacher to pupil and watched as Miss Lefebvre straightened her spine and smiled graciously. Gertrude nodded back and immediately copied Miss Lefebvre's posture and expression. "You are quite right, Mama," she said contritely. "Please do forgive me, Mr. Cormick. I am still learning."

"I think you are doing splendidly," Cormick said gallantly, raising his glass in a toast. Gertrude beamed, delighted at his compliment.

The servants appeared and served them with thick slices of perfectly pink roast beef, a rich meat gravy, crisp roasted potatoes and vegetables from the walled garden. The food was excellent, as always, and conversation grew sparse for a few minutes while everyone took the first few bites, savoring the flavors.

"So, Mr. Cormick, will you be in London for the Season?" Mama asked, as she cut up her meat and then took a dainty bite.

"I shall, your Grace," Cormick said. "I am in London most of the year, now. I have the running of my father's enterprise there."

"He must be very proud of you. I hear business goes well," Mama said with an approving nod. Cormick might not have a title, but his mother was the daughter of an earl and his father was an extremely successful man. He had been doing business with Claveston's father for many years, and Cormick would undoubtedly be seen as a suitable match for Gertrude, with his ten thousand pounds a year and a fine manor house and estate in the neighboring county.

"It does, your Grace, but such talk is not suitable for the dinner table," Cormick said with a polite smile. "I hear you have been traveling around Europe again?"

"I have, and I must leave for the continent again soon," she said without even looking Cormick's way.

Gertrude's pinned-on smile faltered. Claveston reached under the table and squeezed his sister's hand. Mama's appearances were often fleeting. He was used to her comings and goings, and the news fazed him little these days. But he could remember being a boy and how much they had hurt. It infuriated Claveston that his mother so little understood the impact that her leaving again so soon might have upon Gertrude.

A telltale wobble of his sister's bottom lip told him how hurt she was by their mother's bored announcement. "You will not be here for my debut?" Gertrude asked, her usually bold voice faltering.

"I shall be back for your presentation at Court, do not fret," Mama said dismissively. "You will have dear Miss Lefebvre to accompany you through any events before then. She will take excellent care of you. Of that, I have no doubt."

Miss Lefebvre blushed prettily, but Claveston was sure he noted a flash of rage in the young woman's eyes, she was not coloring up because of the compliment, but at the treatment of her charge. He was more than a little incensed himself. Mama had made such a big thing of Gertrude's Coming Out. She had insisted it be this Season, despite Miss Lefebvre's concerns that Gertrude was not yet ready - and had made it seem as though she herself would be at Gertrude's side to smooth her passage through Society. He had been disappointed many times by his mother, but to do such a thing to Gertrude after everything was not right.

CHAPTER NINE

"Mama, do you not think it would be better for Gertrude if you were there to introduce her?" Lord Wycliffe asked, his tone cool, though his jaw was tight as he attempted to hold back his obvious rage at the duchess' announcement. "She will need your intervention to procure the necessary vouchers for Almack's and to be introduced to your friends."

"Miss Lefebvre can do all of that," her Grace said dismissively. "I have had word from my agent that the piece I have been waiting for is to be sold at auction in Paris. I cannot miss it."

"Could you not let your agent act in your stead?" Lord Wycliffe asked pointedly, his frustration with his mother more easily heard in his tone as his ire grew. Sophie was glad that he was speaking up for the poor girl. Someone needed to, and she could not. It was not her place, though she longed to do so.

But Claveston's intervention was heartening, it

showed how much he had changed. But his growth mattered little in this moment. Gertrude had been such a joy since her mama had returned. She had blossomed under the duchess' constant attention and had worked so very hard to please her. It seemed most unfair that the reward Gertrude most needed, to have her mother by her side at the most important time of her life, was to be snatched from her.

"No, I could not," her Grace snapped. "And I'll hear no more about this."

The servants cleared the plates and dessert was brought through. A sculpted sugar-paste confection in the shape of Compton Hall sat upon a mirrored tray, surrounded by *tassses à glace* and a range of crisp sugar biscuits and macarons. Bonnet poured glasses of sweet dessert wine, so they might dip the biscuits and savor the combination of flavors.

But nobody reached for any of it.

The entire room was silent. Gertrude was sulking. Sophie was mortified on the child's behalf. Mr. Cormick looked embarrassed and fidgeted awkwardly next to Sophie. And Lord Wycliffe, well it was quite clear from his tight expression and his flashing eyes, that he was fuming.

"Might I be excused?" Gertrude asked nervously, looking as though she might burst into tears at any moment.

"I don't see why not," the duchess snapped all pretense at politeness now completely gone.

Gertrude ran from the room, raising her hand to her face

as she went to smother her sobs. Sophie was sure that she was crying. She and Lord Wycliffe shared concerned looks. He obviously wanted to go after his sister, to comfort her, but he had a guest to entertain. And his mama would no doubt think him too soft on Gertrude if he were to follow after her.

Sophie too was torn. For the briefest of moments, she felt rooted to the spot. She did not wish to offend the woman at the head of the table. The two women had grown rather fond of one another in the past weeks, and Sophie was most grateful for the duchess' approval of her position. But she could not see Gertrude hurting and leave her to bear it alone. She knew who needed her loyalty more yet feared the repercussions of disappointing the duchess.

Taking a deep breath, she got up from her chair, her decision made. "If you will excuse me," she said bobbing a polite curtsey to the duchess and nodding to the two men, who had risen from their seats as she had. "I should go and assist Lady Gertrude."

She did not wait for permission. Gertrude needed her. No, that wasn't strictly true. Gertrude needed the love and continued attention of her parents. Without it, she lost sight of who she was. But in the absence of that, Sophie was all she had.

Sophie hurried to the girl's chambers, where she found Gertrude staring out of her bedroom window, tears pouring down her cheeks. "Do you know why I chose these rooms, rather than yours?" Gertrude said as Sophie sat beside her on the window seat and took her hand. Sophie shook her head. "Yours are so much finer, but these look out over the driveway. I can see right to the London Road from here," she said sadly.

"So, you can see the arrival of your family, when they return from their many travels," Sophie said understanding the girl's need at once.

"You must think me terribly silly," Gertrude said.

"Not at all," Sophie assured her. "Every girl needs her mother's love, and her father's."

She put her arms around Gertrude's thin shoulders and pulled her into a comforting embrace. Gertrude snaked her arm around Sophie's waist, and they stayed there for some time. When Gertrude pulled away, Sophie pulled out her handkerchief and wiped Gertrude's tears, then tucked a stray strand of the girl's hair back behind her ear. Gertrude gave her a wan smile. "What would I do without you?" she said bleakly.

"You do not need think on that," Sophie assured her. "I promise that I am not going anywhere."

"You mean it? You swear?" Gertrude said desperately.

"I do. I will not leave you, unless you wish me to go. I swear."

The girl snuggled closer, and Sophie sat with her, letting her cry. After some time had passed, Gertrude sat up and pulled away. "I think I would like to go to bed now," Gertrude said, with a yawn. "I am quite exhausted."

"I shall leave you. Would you like me to send up Myrtle to assist you?"

"No, I don't need a lady's maid tonight," Gertrude said sadly. Sophie kissed her on the cheek and left, closing the door softly behind her. Poor Gertrude. All she wanted was to be loved, to be seen even by her mother.

In the days that followed tensions between everyone in Compton Hall made for a very uncomfortable time. The duchess seemed not to notice a thing, blithely continuing with her plans to travel and with the fittings for Gertrude's gowns for the Season. Gertrude was surly with everyone, especially Sophie. At times, Sophie considered that it was just that Sophie was the only person she could take out her frustrations to – but as the days went by, she came to realize that Gertrude was ashamed that Sophie had seen her so upset and had been kind to her.

Gertrude was not the kind of girl to wish to be in debt to anyone she deemed below her station. And Sophie's concern and genuine affection could easily be seen as a debt - one Gertrude did not know how to repay. She had not been taught how to give and accept love freely, other than with her brother. Sophie's ability to love easily was a gift that nobody in the Compton household seemed blessed with. All were entirely too suspicious of other people's motives and considered that there must always be a cost to friendship that must be paid.

The tension was suddenly broken, five days after that uncomfortable dinner party, when a carriage rumbled up the driveway, as Sophie and Gertrude were halfway through a painting lesson, on the lawns at the front of the house. "Papa," Gertrude cried, looking painfully hopeful that somehow her father's arrival might solve all the ills in her young life. She raced after the carriage, barely waiting for it to come to a halt before she opened the door and flung herself inside.

Sophie followed more sedately and bobbed a curtsey to the Duke of Compton, who peered out at her over the shoulder of his sobbing daughter. "Might I ask why my daughter is so very emotional?" he asked.

"She is just glad to see you, your Grace," Sophie said. It was true enough. "Come Lady Gertrude, let your father at least leave his carriage and come inside."

Gertrude released him reluctantly and stepped down from the carriage. She stood demurely next to Sophie and offered her father a deep curtsey. He nodded his approval. "I see you have had some influence then," he said with a wry smile. "But it is quite clear that my daughter is still a hoyden."

He got out of the carriage and put an arm around his daughter's waist. She snuck her arm around his and the two of them walked towards the house together, talking animatedly about all the gifts and treasures that he had brought back from America and the Indies for her. Sophie marveled at how much the duke and duchess seemed to genuinely love their daughter, when they could be bothered to do so - yet did not seem to see that she did not need their gifts, or their money. All Gertrude wanted was them, their love, and their time.

As they reached the doors, the sound of hoofbeats behind them made all three of them turn back to the driveway. Mr. Cormick approached at a gallop, his tail-coat flapping in the wind behind him. He grinned at them all as he dismounted and ran up the stone steps, two at a time. "I am glad to have caught you, your Grace," he said bowing deeply to the duke and then to Sophie and Gertrude.

"What is it, young Cormick?" his Grace asked.

"My father asked if he might wait upon you, at your nearest convenience," Mr. Cormick said. "He has some matters of great import he must discuss with you. Has been waiting for your return for some weeks. As soon as we got word that you were back in England, he sent me here and my brother to your London house, to be sure that you received the message straight away."

Gertrude's expression sank. Sophie moved to comfort her, but the young woman moved away. She clenched her delicate fingers into fists, then raced inside and up the stairs. "Whatever is the matter with her?" his Grace asked but did not wait for an answer. He turned back to Mr. Cormick. "Is he in town, or in Hertfordshire?"

"In town, your Grace."

"Then I shall have the horses changed and head there straight away." Cormick nodded. "Take your mount to the stables, have him fed and rubbed down. Take one of Claveston's to return to London and inform your father that I shall be there shortly." Cormick bowed to the duke, and Sophie and did as he had been told.

"And you, Miss Lefebvre," the duke said, turning to her. "Might I speak with you in my study, before I depart?"

Sophie bobbed a curtsey. "Of course, your Grace," she said.

She wondered what it was he wished to say to her. Her stomach began to churn as she followed him into the wood-paneled study and took the seat opposite his desk when he indicated she should sit. "Miss Lefebvre," the duke said, clasping his hands in front of him on the desk and looking at her frankly. "I have been assured, by both my son and my wife, that you have been doing an excellent job of preparing my daughter for her debut. However, that display of temper that I have just witnessed leads me to think otherwise. Do you have an explanation?"

Sophie stared at him, open-mouthed. Somehow, she was the one at fault for Gertrude's behavior? Gertrude had been in perfect control of her emotions, or at least she had been able to control them better, until her parents had flown back into her lives with their ready promises of love and affection, and both were now withdrawing themselves once more. She knew that it was not her place to comment, to point out the glaring reason why Gertrude was so upset, yet she fumed silently that she was to be made out as the one to be blamed.

"Miss Lefebvre," the duke continued when she did not speak. "You come highly recommended. Your time with Lady Charlotte Watts is a great credit to you. I am told that Gertrude has learned much under your tutelage. But I must stress to you, that her Coming Out is of great importance. Of all people, you must realize that her chances of making a suitable match are greatly enhanced by the success of her debut."

Sophie forced herself to ignore the insinuation that as she was herself still unmarried and that must somehow mean that she had been at fault when she had been Gertrude's age. "I am aware," she said trying to keep her tone even. "I can assure you that Gertrude is ready."

"I should hope so. If she fails, it will be your responsibility, Miss Lefebvre."

"I understand," Sophie said through gritted teeth. "Is that all, your Grace?"

"For now," the duke said, waving his hand dismissively. Sophie stood up, curtseyed, and then let herself out of the room.

She hurried outside and away from the house, into the woods where she let out a most unladylike scream. How dare he? How dare either of them try and blame her for their daughter's unhappiness? She paced up and down, her fists clenched, and her jaw set as she tried to let go the anger that she was suddenly feeling towards both the Duke and Duchess of Compton. They treated their children as playthings, picking them up and discarding them at will, then wondered why they were so spoiled and willful.

Mr. Cormick appeared, running through the trees, looking breathless. "I heard a scream," he said, looking around. "Are you quite alright?"

"I am quite well," she assured him. "I am not hurt. Simply angry."

"Ah," he said knowingly. "Yes, I've seen Wycliff struggling his whole life to deal with the peculiarities of his family."

"How can they be so blind?" Sophie asked him. "Do they choose not to see how much their absences and whirlwind trips hurt Lord Wycliffe and Lady Gertrude?"

"You have been around the English aristocracy long enough to know that children are heirs and a means to extend one's holdings, Miss Lefebvre. Love is not part of the deal in many families in Society. Marriage is as much a business transaction as any done in the City, and often has more at stake. Producing an heir and a spare is a duty, not a choice."

"I know it should not shock me. But somehow it still does," Sophie said. "I was aware that Lord William and Lady Charlotte's father was distant and demanding, but I suppose I assumed that was because the duke was grieving for his wife and 'ad never quite managed to get over her dying. I excused his behavior, I suppose."

"Nothing to excuse," Mr. Cormick said with a grin. "All perfectly normal. Showing affection would be the more unusual behavior."

"Are your parents the same?"

"Thankfully, no. But theirs was a love match, and we are not quite so wealthy and powerful. To be a duke is a heavy burden."

"I can imagine," Sophie said.

She glanced along the path, back towards the house. A lone figure stood in the formal gardens, facing their way. She was sure it was Lord Wycliffe, yet he came no closer. She wondered how long he had been watching them. "I should go inside and check on Lady Gertrude," she said, as he turned away and stomped back towards the house.

"And I should be on my way," Mr. Cormick said, as always honoring her with a bow. "It was my pleasure to see you again, Miss Lefebvre. And try not to let them get to you. Underneath it all, they are all kind and good people."

"I am sure you are right," Sophie said, letting him kiss

her hand as they reached the house. She watched as he headed back towards the stables, then went inside. She wasn't quite sure she would ever understand the peculiarities of the English, no matter how long she lived amongst them.

CHAPTER TEN

C laveston spoke only briefly with his father before the duke got back into his carriage and returned to London. Mrs. Grint caught him in the hallway as his father's carriage crunched out of sight and told him of the scene with Gertrude, and the duke's private talk with Miss Lefebvre in his study. She had also told him that Miss Lefebvre had hurried away from the house looking just as upset as his sister had been before her. He had dithered for a moment, wondering which of the young women he should go to first.

He glanced outside and heard a scream. He rushed towards it, then stopped as he saw Cormick heading in the same direction. Claveston stood perfectly still as he watched his friend greet Miss Lefebvre. He waited, expecting them both to return to the house. Miss Lefebvre would not speak alone in the woods with a gentleman. She knew better than to risk her reputation that way. But time ticked by and still they talked together, smiling and laughing. He felt a surge of fury course through him. He had not welcomed Cormick into his home, for him to get in the way of Claveston's intentions towards Miss Lefebvre.

But what were his intentions? Claveston knew he liked her. He knew that she was nothing like any woman he had ever known before. She was unfazed by his wealth and position. She cared nothing for possessions and displays of grandeur. She liked the simple things, a good book, a fine meal, and good company. It was no wonder she enjoyed talking with Cormick. The man was the most genial companion Claveston had – and he was unaffected by his father's wealth and status, and the expectations upon him, though he had no title and no estate to inherit. As he watched his friend and the woman he was coming to love, he was envious of them both. They would make a fine match.

He turned on his heel and went back inside. His sister needed him, even if Miss Lefebvre did not. Gertrude had been doing so well, up until his mother had announced her imminent departure. To have Papa return home and then turn around and leave immediately would have been too much for her to bear. He rushed up the stairs and found her peering out of the window in Miss Lefebvre's parlor, looking out over the formal gardens, down towards the woods. She had red, puffy eyes and streaks upon her cheeks.

"What are you doing in here?" he asked her as he sat down and hugged her tightly. "These are Miss Lefebvre's private chambers."

"I know. I saw her run out of the house from my own window. She headed this way," Gertrude said, nodding towards the woodland. "She looked very upset."

"I believe Papa spoke with her before he left," Claveston said, rolling his eyes.

"Oh, poor Miss Lefebvre," Gertrude said. "He no doubt blamed her for my bad behavior."

"I am sure he probably did," Claveston agreed. "Are you quite alright, little one? You must have been so excited to see him."

"I was," Gertrude admitted. "And I so wanted Mama to be with me in London, and she is leaving tomorrow. Did she tell you?"

Claveston shook his head. He'd not seen the duchess since dinner last night, and she'd certainly made no mention of it then. "You do know, you will always have me, don't you?" he assured her. "I will always be nearby if you need me – and if I am away, all you need do is send for me."

"I do," Gertrude said, but it didn't sound like she believed him. "And I have Sophie." She paused and glanced back out of the window again, to where Sophie and Cormick had been talking just moments earlier. "Do you think she will stay? She seems awfully friendly with Mr. Cormick."

Claveston sighed heavily. They were back to this once more. Poor Gertrude. All she had ever known was people leaving her as soon as she grew fond of them. "I do not think you need worry about that. Miss Lefebvre is friendly to everyone, and Cormick, well I am certain he has no intentions of stealing her away from you. She is very fond of you, and we are both extremely proud of all you have accomplished, you know."

Gertrude squirmed away from him. "I do." She peered out of the window again. "She promised she wouldn't leave me. Perhaps I should go and check on her?"

"I'm sure she is quite alright," Claveston assured her. "You wash your face and put on a pretty dress, then come downstairs. Perhaps we can play some croquet?"

"I should like that; it is such a lovely day. I should fetch my paints and my easel, too. We were painting the house when Papa arrived. I completely forgot. They are most likely still there."

"That would be a great help to Miss Lefebvre," Claveston said standing up and then pressing a kiss to her forehead.

Claveston made his way downstairs and fetched the croquet set from the hallway cupboard. It was hidden beneath the grand staircase and was full of all manner of sporting equipment, parasols, and other items that the family used when the weather was fine.

He went outside and began setting up the hoops on the lawn. Gertrude soon followed him outside, and true to her word, tidied away her art materials first before she joined him on the lawn. She bounced back outside. "I have ordered lemonade for us," she said as she took a mallet from him. One of the footmen followed her, carrying a small cast iron table, and the kitchen lad followed on with two chairs.

"I tried to find Miss Lefebvre, to ask if she cared to join us, but I cannot find her anywhere," Gertrude said, as she indicated where her helpers should set down their load.

"That is a shame, but it is rather nice to have you all to myself for an hour or two," Claveston said.

They began their game. Croquet was one of Gertrude's favorite pastimes. She was fiercely competitive, and Claveston wasn't entirely sure that she wasn't of a mind to cheat when the need arose. But they enjoyed a spirited game, that his sister won by a whisker. He congratulated her, then noticed that Miss Lefebvre was heading towards them with a tray of refreshments. He hurried to help her. "Are you alright?" he asked her as he took the tray from her.

"I am," she assured him. "Mr. Cormick was kind enough to check on me."

"He seems quite partial to you," Claveston said, trying to sound as if such a thing made no difference to him.

"He 'as been most kind, but I do not think there is anything more to it than that," Miss Lefebvre said as they drew near to Gertrude.

Claveston set the tray down upon the table, and Gertrude immediately helped herself to a glass of lemonade. She gulped it down without thinking. Sophie frowned at her as she set the glass back onto the tray. "I know, I know," Gertrude said rolling her eyes. "I should have waited for Claveston to pull out my seat, and until everyone else was seated before I offered to serve them first. But I am fashed, and it is so hot this afternoon."

It was Claveston's turn to frown at her this time. "And I know I shouldn't say fashed," she said. Claveston and Miss Lefebvre couldn't help themselves, they both started to giggle. "What?" Gertrude demanded, looking put out that she seemed to be the butt of their joke.

"It is that you know precisely what you should do, yet you still do the opposite," Claveston said fondly. "It is of no mind when it is just us, but you must remember when you are in London, Gertrude."

"I know," Gertrude said in a mocking sing-song tone. "Or I shall damage the family name and all my prospects for a good marriage."

"Are you mocking Mama?" Claveston said, pretending to be aghast.

"Perhaps a little," Gertrude admitted. "I am sick of hearing it, over and over."

"Well, I care little for any damage you do to the family name," he assured her. "But I do care for any you might do to your own, or to Miss Lefebvre's."

"You are right, of course. I should never wish to hurt Sophie," Gertrude said, turning to her with wide eyes. "She has been the perfect companion."

They all smiled, but Claveston could see that Miss Lefebvre was both touched and slightly embarrassed by the praise. "Well, if you are fashed, dear sister, perhaps I should challenge Miss Lefebvre to a match?"

"Perhaps you should," she said, pouring herself another glass of lemonade and sitting down at the table. "Sophie, you must beat him. He can be a terrible bore if he wins."

"I shall try my best," Miss Lefebvre said with a gentle smile.

Playing croquet with Miss Lefebvre was a pleasure.

She was not so openly competitive as Gertrude, but she went about her business with quiet competence, and Claveston was surprised to find himself quite a ways behind. It didn't help that she looked so perfectly intent when she lined up her mallet to the ball, looking carefully from the ball to the hoop and back, adjusting her stance and her grip, then striking the ball cleanly.

Gertrude had kept up her incessant chatter through the early part of the game, but she seemed to have grown bored, and was glancing around the gardens, as if looking for something or someone more interesting. Claveston wondered if she would ever truly master the skills a young lady needed to possess in Society. She was too impatient, too unruly. Unlike Miss Lefebvre, who made it all look so effortless. She was so graceful at whatever she did. She knew when to duck her head or shield her eyes. She painted better than many artists whose work Claveston had seen in the galleries of some of the finest homes in the country. And she played the pianoforte so beautifully that he could hardly bear it.

"Sit up straight," he called to Gertrude. She scowled, stuck out her tongue at him, and continued to slouch.

"She knows not to do such things in company," Miss Lefebvre assured him. "I 'ave no concerns for her, other than her temperament."

"She is a little fiery," Claveston agreed. "She is too used to getting her own way. She does not take well to direction – and I think sometimes she gets angry simply to get our attention."

"I think you may be quite right," Miss Lefebvre

agreed. "I think much of her behavior is an attempt to be seen by those who may never truly see her."

"Our parents."

"Indeed."

"They will not ever change," Claveston said with a heavy sigh. "At some point, Gertrude must learn to bear that."

"I agree, but it is not a lesson that I can teach her," Miss Lefebvre said sadly. "It is something she will learn, in time. At least, I hope she will. Perhaps, she will find someone who will love her enough to make up for all of it."

"He'd need the patience of a saint," Claveston joked.

"No, just a warm heart," Miss Lefebvre said softly.

Their game continued, and Claveston began to catch up as Miss Lefebvre made some silly mistakes. He teased her and they laughed about it, all the while, Gertrude looked more and more bored. She stood up. "I think I should go inside. I did not bring a parasol, and Mama would be most upset if my skin were to get too dark."

Claveston suppressed the urge to tell her off. He had been genuinely enjoying the afternoon and now it would need to be cut short, as it would be improper for him to remain out here alone with Miss Lefebvre. Yet, she was right. Mama would be most annoyed if her daughter arrived in London looking like a servant girl, her skin dark from the sun.

"I shall see to it that everything is brought inside," he assured Miss Lefebvre, who had moved towards the table and was tidying the plates and glasses onto the tray.

"Thank you," she said and followed her young charge inside.

Claveston stood still for a few moments, just watching her walk. Her hips swayed ever so slightly, her steps light – as if she was walking on air. He had barely noticed how much she had come to mean to him since she had been here. He had admired her from the first, when they met at Lord Cott's marriage to Lady Mary. He had realized what a treasure she would be to his household when they'd met again at Watton Hall at Christmas. But he had not known that she would creep into his heart so easily.

Miss Sophie Lefebvre would make him a perfect wife. She had all the attributes, and more, that his parents might demand in a bride for him. She was beautiful, sweet, kind, and clever. She behaved impeccably in almost every situation. He chuckled as he remembered her dressing Lady Honoria down all those weeks ago. She had been unhappy in that company, and she had not cared if they approved of her or not – and so she had done what any good friend should and had stood by those she loved.

She had made him realize that he wasn't as good a friend as he should be – because it should have been him saying those things. He knew that he would never be so timid now. He knew that he did not need the approval of any member of *the Ton* – because the only person's approval he would ever seek, would be hers.

CHAPTER ELEVEN

G ertrude was unusually quiet at dinner and went up to bed having barely uttered a word to Sophie, or her mother. She spoke tersely with Lord Wycliffe, but it seemed that whatever he said to her, only worsened the girl's mood. Her emotions were becoming more mercurial by the day, and Sophie wished there was something that she could do to help the poor girl to cope with the things that troubled her.

The duchess also retired early, citing her long journey the next day as the reason. It left Sophie and Lord Wycliffe in an uncomfortable position, as they sat at the dining table alone. "I should go, too," Sophie said getting up from her chair.

Lord Wycliffe caught her arm as she passed his chair. "Please don't," he asked, his dark eyes soft. "I should hate to have to take my port alone in the library. I could have Bonnet bring it in here, if you would agree to stay and talk with me."

"I should go, it would not be seemly," Sophie argued,

but her words rang false even to her. What harm could there be, in a room with servants all around them?

"I could send for Mrs. Grint?" Lord Wycliffe said with a grin, obviously understanding the reason for her reticence.

Sophie shook her head and sat back down. "That won't be necessary. She 'as more than enough to be getting on with, without acting as my chaperone. We are suitably accompanied by James and Holly, are we not?" She smiled at the young footman and parlor maid that had been acting as their servers that evening. Both gave her shy grins in return.

Lord Wycliffe smile contentedly. Yet again he had gotten his way, though in many ways, so had she. She was not yet weary enough for bed, and an evening alone in her room with no company but a book did not appeal. "What do you normally do, when Lady Gertrude and I retire, my Lord?" she asked him curiously.

He grinned. "I read, sometimes I work on the estate ledgers. Occasionally, I drink port and smoke a cigar out on the terrace."

"Does that not bore you? I rather got the impression that you enjoyed parties and the high life."

"Oh, I do," Claveston said. "But I appreciate them all the more when I have spent enough time here being quiet." He paused. His eyes sought hers and Sophie felt as though he was looking right into her soul. "I get the feeling that such pastimes are not to your liking?"

"It is not that, my Lord," Sophie said. "I enjoy company, but I am fond of rather less boisterous affairs I think, than perhaps those you are used to."

"Such as the Watts' Christmas Eve party?" Lord Wycliffe asked with a smile.

"Precisely," she said. "I like to be able to hear myself think, to know what the person next to me is actually saying – and to be able to know everyone present and not need to be introduced."

"You are going to struggle in London, aren't you?" he asked, concern in his eyes.

"If I am honest, I do not know," Sophie admitted. "I had a London season when I was eighteen. I enjoyed the whirl of dancing and being seen then, but now I am older, per'aps a little quieter, I am not looking forward to our time there, especially, but I shall do my duty by your sister."

"I don't doubt it," Lord Wycliffe said with a chuckle. "She is lucky to have you. But are you glad that you came to us, here at Compton I mean? I know that it is in large part down to my pushing you that you did so, Miss Lefebvre."

Sophie thought for a moment before answering. It was not a straightforward question, and the way Lord Wycliffe was looking at her now made it even harder. It was quite clear to Sophie that he wanted her to be happy. He wanted to know that she had no regrets. He cared for her, and her happiness. She was not sure how she knew that, but in that moment, she did.

"I am content enough," she said eventually. "My work is enjoyable. Lady Gertrude is a dear thing, most of the time."

They both laughed at that. But they were so caught up in their conversation, so fascinated with one another, that they hadn't heard the sound of footsteps in the hall-way, or the creak of the door as Gertrude had crept back downstairs and listened to their conversation. She clutched at the doorframe, her knuckles turning white as she heard them laughing at her and her anger at everyone grew and grew.

"Do you not tire of all the formality between us, Miss Lefebvre?" Lord Wycliffe asked. "You may call me Claveston, if you wish."

"I could not," Sophie protested. "I am your sister's companion. It is right that I observe the proprieties."

"Not even when we are alone?" he pressed. "Try it, see how it sounds." His dark eyes were full of teasing, and Sophie flushed at the attention he was bestowing upon her. She had once thought him arrogant and self-centered. But she had come to see that he was, in many ways, as damaged as his dear sister. He merely wished to be liked.

"Claveston," Sophie said, trying out his name.

"I like the way it sounds," he said. "Your accent makes it sound so much more romantic that it normally does."

"You should not tease me," Sophie said sternly. "I cannot 'elp the way I speak."

"I am not teasing you," he said earnestly. "I should never wish to tease you, dear Sophie – if I may call you Sophie?"

She nodded, her stomach suddenly a mass of roiling and writhing snakes. This moment was too personal, too intimate – even with the servants present. It would not be right for her to let things go any further. Gertrude needed her. She had been afraid from the first of an attraction between Sophie and her brother. Sophie had promised her that such a thing could never be - and had meant it.

But she had thought Claveston to be a very different man then. Even if he had professed his undying love to her when she first arrived, she would not have entertained it. But she had learned that the face he presented to the world was not the man underneath. The real Claveston was kind, gentle, and sweet. He was also rather shy in his own way. He did not trust anyone to like him for himself, and like dear Gertrude, he expected everyone to turn away from him eventually.

"Sophie, I am so glad you came to Compton," he said now, reaching across the table and taking her hand. Sophie snatched it away and jumped to her feet.

"My Lord, you should not," she said. "And if you insist upon acting this way, then I must bid you good night."

She swept from the room and ran up to her rooms, where she slammed the door behind her and turned the key. She was too confused by what had just happened. She had not come to Compton expecting to find love. She had given up on that a long time ago. Yet it appeared that Sophie's heart had not gotten the message. She still longed for a husband and a family of her own – and she wanted that husband to be Claveston St. John, Earl of Wycliffe.

THE MEMORY of those brief moments in the dining room with Sophie kept Claveston smiling all through the next day, despite having to attend quarter day to take the rents for the estate. He chatted with the tenants, and listened to their grievances, offering counsel where he could, assistance where required, and promised to ask his father about the things he could not decide upon there and then.

He returned home to Compton Hall in the late afternoon, to find Mrs. Grint waiting for him in the hallway. "What is it?" he asked, taking one look at her worried face, and assuming the worst. "Is it Gertrude? Please don't tell me she went riding alone and had an accident?"

"No, everyone is quite well – at least physically," the housekeeper assured him. "No, it is your father." She paused.

"Has he returned?"

"Yes, first thing this morning. Not long after you left, my Lord," Mrs. Grint said nervously.

"So, he arrived before Mama had left?" Claveston asked, knowing where this might be going. The housekeeper nodded. "And he insisted she not go, which put Mama in a snit?"

"She was furious, my Lord."

"I cannot say I am not glad. Gertrude will need Mama in London. It isn't right that she intended to go traveling again at such an important time for my sister."

"But that is not all, my Lord," Mrs. Grint said, her eyes darting towards the closed door of his father's study. "They are both in there now, with Miss Lefebvre."

"With Sophie? But why?" Claveston demanded.

"Because her Grace discovered that a piece of very expensive jewelry, one of your grandmother's pieces I believe, is missing," Mrs. Grint explained.

"I still don't understand what that has to do with Sophie," Claveston said striding across the hallway to the study, then it dawned on him. "They think she took it?" Mrs. Grint nodded.

Claveston rolled his eyes and barged into the study without knocking. He had never heard anything so ridiculous in his life. His father was sitting behind his desk, his face puce with rage. Mama sat primly on a chair to his side, glaring at poor Miss Lefebvre who was staring at the floor, her voice tight and quiet. "I cannot tell you how it came to be in my armoire," she was saying. "I only know I did not do this. I would never do such a thing. You must believe me."

"Father, you cannot truly believe that Miss Lefebvre would do such a thing?" Claveston demanded.

"I do not know what to think," his father said. "I do not know the woman."

"I can assure you that she would never steal, or lie," Claveston went on. "She is the sweetest, kindest, most generous woman I have ever met. I have never known anyone less interested in wealth and jewels in my life. She simply could not have done this."

"Yet the tiara was found in her chambers," Mama said brusquely. "If she did not put it there, then who did?"

"I do not know, but Miss Lefebvre spent nine years in the employ of the Duchy of Mormont. Do you not think that if she had such inclinations that they would have been evident in all that time?" Claveston was fuming.

"Perhaps she was simply better at hiding her sins there," Mama said spitefully. "We should send her before the magistrate and see what he makes of it all. I don't doubt he'd have her hanging from a noose for such a brazen act." Miss Lefebvre blanched at Mama's words, and Claveston clenched his fists hard enough to turn his knuckles white as he tried to control his anger.

He could hardly believe how quickly his mother's feelings towards Miss Lefebvre seemed to have changed. He had thought his mother had developed a genuine affection for her daughter's companion. They had so often conversed in French together, and Mama had seemed to truly like Miss Lefebvre. He knew his mother could be distant, but such a swift turnabout was disconcerting.

He glanced at Miss Lefebvre. Her bottom lip was trembling, and she was fighting the urge to cry so hard that it broke his heart. She could barely bring herself to look him in the eye. "Father, if I may be so bold, perhaps we should look into this more closely before we make a hasty judgment that we might later regret."

"What do you suggest?" the duke asked caustically. "Everything seems quite straightforward to me. Your mother is quite right, the woman should be in front of a magistrate."

"Perhaps, Miss Lefebvre might remain in her rooms until we can question the entire household. Perhaps somebody saw something. There is always someone watching in this household. The servants always know everything," Claveston said, not expecting his father to agree, but he had to do something.

Surprisingly, the duke nodded his head. "It would be wise to be sure of the facts before we turn anyone out of the house," he agreed. "Though I don't know what you think questioning them all will turn up. But the magistrate will want to know the full story, so it may be for the best."

Mama frowned. "I want this matter sorted swiftly," she warned Claveston. "I intended to leave Compton today. I will not delay my trip longer than a week."

The duke rang a bell. Mrs. Grint knocked on the door and entered with a curtsey. "Yes, your Grace?"

"Take Miss Lefebvre to her chambers. She will remain there until Claveston has looked into this matter. Ensure that no member of staff leaves this house until they have been questioned. They are to make themselves available as soon as my son requests them."

"Yes, your Grace," Mrs. Grint said. Sophie stood and followed the elderly housekeeper into the hallway.

"You have three days," the duke said sternly. "If we know no more by then, I will turn her over to the local magistrate."

"I understand," Claveston said, bowed and left the room.

He hurried after Mrs. Grint and Sophie. He caught up with them on the stairs. "I shall find who did this, Miss Lefebvre," he assured her. "I will clear your good name. I promise you that."

She nodded but didn't say a word. Mrs. Grint put an arm around her shoulder and escorted her upstairs.

Claveston frowned as he turned to look back at his parents who had emerged from Papa's study and were watching him with narrowed eyes.

Neither of them looked happy. Claveston wondered if it was because of what had happened, or that his intervention would force them to spend time in each other's company. When he was young, they had traveled together. They had seemed to be so in love that they couldn't bear to be apart. Yet, as the years had gone on, they had grown further and further away from one another. He could count on one hand the number of times that they had been here at Compton together in the past five years. How had their marriage come to that, he wondered?

He was used to them arguing, ignoring one another – and avoiding each other. Yet, for once, they were agreed on something. Whoever had stolen the tiara needed to be punished. And they would not hesitate to see that person hang, though no harm had been done and the tiara had been recovered. Claveston prayed that his investigations would prove that it wasn't Sophie, because he couldn't bear the thought of her having to face such an end. She was so much better than any of them and he was sure that she was as innocent as he knew himself to be.

CHAPTER TWELVE

The hours passed so slowly as Sophie remained in her room, waiting for news. The duchess had insisted Sophie not even go out into the grounds or to spend any time with Gertrude, so she was all alone. At first, she had ranted and railed, sobbed and fumed. But now, she was spent. She could not believe that anyone in this house could do such a thing to her – because she knew that she was innocent. Whoever had placed that tiara in her armoire must truly hate her, and that thought upset Sophie greatly.

Nobody came to visit her. Mrs. Grint brought her meals up but didn't ever stay long. She knew that the housekeeper believed her that she hadn't done it, but it would not be right for Sophie to ask the older woman to stand by her. Mrs. Grint had worked in this house since she was a girl. Her loyalties had to stay with the family she had cared for so diligently and for so long.

By the second day of her luxurious imprisonment, Sophie had calmed enough to read the book she kept by her bedside, but it was not a long book and so it did not take her long to finish it. She did not know what else to do with herself. She wrote in her journal, trying to make sense of it all, and wondering who had actually taken the tiara, and why they had wished Sophie to take the blame.

About an hour before dinner, a gentle knock on the door surprised her. "Enter," she said nervously.

Lord Wycliffe's handsome face peered around the door. He gave her a wan smile. "How are you?" he asked as he pushed the door wide and came inside, followed by Mrs. Grint, who stood quietly in the corner of the room. Lord Wycliffe must have asked her to accompany him to protect Sophie's reputation.

"I 'ave been better," she admitted. "Do you have any news? Anything at all? You must know that I did not do this."

"Of course, I know you did not do it – but I have to prove that to my parents," he said, his eyes full of concern for her.

"Then what can I do?" she said, wringing her hands and pacing up and down.

"You can start by telling me everything that happened that day, and even in the days beforehand. Is there anything that was unusual, or did you see anyone acting suspiciously?"

HE SAT down in the chair by her desk and pulled out a sheet of paper and picked up her pen and dipped it in the ink well. Sophie perched on the edge of her bed and thought carefully. "I 'ave been running through everything, over and over," she said. "I cannot think of anything strange in my day."

"It need not be very strange, but perhaps a second pair of eyes might see something you have not."

Sophie moved to the desk and stood beside him. She bent to the drawer and opened it. She pulled out her journal and opened it to the page where she had written down every minute of that day. He took it and began to read as Sophie paced up and down, biting at the skin around her nails.

"So, you got up that morning at seven," he read. "You washed and dressed, without the assistance of a maid - so you were alone, and nobody can vouch for your where-abouts at that time?" He frowned.

"That is correct," Sophie admitted. Lord Wycliffe sounded so serious, and it made her nervous. "But I was in my rooms. I am always in my rooms at that time of day – as is the entire 'ousehold."

"Please, don't worry, Miss Lefebvre," Lord Wycliffe said, trying to reassure her. "I am just trying to see if there is a time when you were alone and access to the tiara might have been possible. I have asked everyone the same questions. I promise, I am not trying to trip you up."

Sophie nodded, but she felt like a criminal. She had done nothing wrong, yet she was already being punished for the crime. The past few days had been amongst the worst she'd ever spent in her life. She hated that anyone in this house, but especially Lord Wycliffe and Gertrude might think her capable of stealing from them.

"Did you go down to breakfast as normal?" he asked her, gently.

"I did, at eight o'clock," Sophie said, tears pricking at her eyes. "Gertrude was in the dining room before me. We both ate and then agreed to meet in the garden at nine o'clock to take the air. We walked for perhaps two hours, as we normally do, then changed our clothes for lunch."

"So, there was little time when you were alone all morning?"

"No more than five minutes at any point. Only when I dressed for lunch was I alone longer, and then it was not long enough to get changed and to the other end of the house to the duchess' chambers," Sophie said pointedly.

Lord Wycliffe nodded. "I know that," he assured her. "And after lunch?"

Sophie sighed and sank down onto the bed again. "I went straight to the music room for Gertrude's piano lesson. She wanted me to teach her some Beethoven."

"And she came with you to the music room?"

"She did..." Sophie paused. "No, no, she didn't. That day she was a little late. She said she 'ad forgotten some ribbons she wanted to sew onto her gown later that afternoon. She said that she went to her room to fetch them."

"She is often late, and often forgets things, so we may probably discount that as being anything to be concerned about," Lord Wycliffe said with a wry smile. "Yet, how late was she?"

"Per'aps fifteen, maybe twenty minutes." Sophie forced herself to smile wanly back. She had replayed the day over and over again in her mind, and it was the only thing that was in any way unusual – but Lord Wycliffe was probably right, it wasn't unusual enough to warrant suspicion. And what possible reason would Gertrude have for stealing her mother's jewels anyway? The girl had access to whatever she wanted, whenever she wanted. All she ever needed to do was ask.

"I am stumped," Lord Wycliffe admitted, setting down the pen and looking gravely at Sophie. "I have interviewed almost every single servant, every merchant that came to the house, and have peppered my family with questions. There is not a single piece of evidence I can find that proves you did take it – nor one that proves you did not."

"I wish that were not true," Sophie admitted. "I know I did not do this. Even if I was such a person, I 'ad no time to do such a thing."

"I know you did not. But I don't know who did. And I have to tell my father what I have found out. I am afraid he will not be best pleased – and I do not know if I can convince him of your innocence. The most I might be able to convince him of will be to let you go, and not to demand to see you before the magistrate." His eyes were full of despair, though he was trying his best to remain calm and positive for her sake.

"You 'ave tried your best," Sophie said. "I am grateful for that at least. But I shall pack my bags and prepare to leave. Whatever the outcome of this matter, it is inconceivable that I can remain in my position here." Lord Wycliffe bowed himself out of the room, his shoulders hunched, the weight of the world resting upon them.

Mrs. Grint remained behind. "I'm sorry," she said sadly. "It is not right that you should have to leave when you've done nothing wrong."

"You believe me?" Sophie asked. She had not thought anyone other than Lord Wycliffe did. The housekeeper had been so resolutely silent until now, her expression always giving nothing away.

"Of course, I do," Mrs. Grint said firmly. "I know your character. You'd never do such a thing. There's people in this house as might, but not amongst the staff."

Sophie was surprised at her comment. It seemed that the housekeeper was pointing a finger towards someone in the family – but what reason could any of them have for doing such a thing? "What do you mean?"

"We've talked on it before, when a child is starved of love and showered with possessions, they don't develop the values they should."

"You think Lady Gertrude did this? Lord Wycliffe?"

"I cannot say, but the young mistress is the most likely, do you not think?" Mrs. Grint paused for a moment. "She wasn't where she should be, and it took longer than it should to do what she said she was doing? She is a difficult child, always has been. She is used to holding her brother's heart in her hands, and your being here has distracted him from her."

"It 'as not," Sophie protested. Lord Wycliffe had been kind. He had perhaps even flirted with her from time to time, but there was nothing more to his attentions than that. Gertrude would surely not have been so put out by such a fragile acquaintanceship, would she?

"Oh, my dear, it has," Mrs. Grint said with a wry smile. "Anyone with eyes can see how enamored the young lord is with you – and though you have tried to hide your feelings, I've seen them growing. Gertrude would have seen it, too. She's no fool, that child for all her willfulness."

"She is very observant," Sophie noted. "But you are wrong. There is nothing between Lord Wycliffe and myself." She didn't dare hope that the housekeeper was right. It would make the fact she must now leave this house even more unbearable.

"Whatever you say," Mrs. Grint said. "The truth will out, though it may be too late for you by then. And for that, I am very sad. You have been good for Lady Gertrude, and Lord Claveston. They both need you in their own way."

"It is what it is," Sophie said, sadly. "I can bear it. The people that matter know I did not do this. That is at least some kind of comfort I 'ave some money saved, will be able to afford to support myself for a time, if Lord Wycliffe can convince his parents not to send me to the gallows" Mrs. Grint winced at the words. Sophie gave her a resigned smile. "Perhaps he might be able to 'elp me get back to France."

"I shall miss you," Mrs. Grint said.

"Thank you, it is kind of you to say so."

"Do not forget what you have achieved here, even if your leaving feels like a failure. You have changed them both, but especially Lord Claveston. The boy I knew would not be doing what the man today is attempting. He would never have stood up to his father, would never have taken the harder side in any battle. He's always been one for an easy life, but he's gone out of his way for you."

"He would do the same for you, or for Bonnet, I am sure."

"No, he wouldn't, or at least he wouldn't have done so before he met you. I believe he might do now. He's finally become the fine young man I tried to raise him to be."

Sophie glanced around the opulent room that had always felt a little too much. "I shall miss this house, Lady Gertrude and you in particular," she said sadly.

"And we'll miss you," Mrs. Grint said. "But I think there's someone who'll miss you more than anyone." She nodded towards the door that Lord Wycliffe had so recently departed through. "He loves you, though I don't know if he knows it yet."

"He does not love me," Sophie said firmly. "And even if he did, there is nothing that could come of it now."

"But you wish it could be otherwise?" Mrs. Grint gave her a knowing look. "I've seen the two of you."

"There is nothing," Sophie protested, but too vehemently. Mrs. Grint laughed. "So, what does it matter if I admit it," Sophie said with a shake of her head. "I 'ave come to care very much for him. It will be hard to say goodbye."

"For him, too."

"He will forget me soon enough."

"No, I don't think he will. I've never seen him this way about anyone. He truly loves you."

"And I love him," Sophie said with a sigh. "But I will be banished and that will be that."

CHAPTER THIRTEEN

Claveston had not slept a wink all that night. He rose early and made his way to the stables. Perhaps a long ride might help him clear his head, and spot whatever it was that he was missing. He had spoken with every single member of the household. He had questioned every one of them at length about their actions that day. He had checked each one of their statements against those of the other staff and found that every single account matched where it should.

He had until the end of the day, and every second of that time seemed to be ticking loudly inside his head. How could he uncover the truth? It must be staring him in the face, and yet he could not see it for looking.

"My Lord," a voice called after him as Claveston strode through the stable yard. "My Lord!" it called again, though louder this time.

"What?" Claveston stormed as he turned to see Watkins, one of the stable lads, running after him, then shook his head. "I'm sorry, lad, did not mean to take out my temper on you."

"My Lord, Jeanie Green is back today," Watkins said panting hard, bending over as he tried to get his breath back. Claveston looked at him blankly. "She's one of the parlor maids, you've not talked to her yet as she was at home, her mother just had another babe, and Jeanie went to help her out a bit. She was here the day the tiara went missing but has been away from the Hall for the past week. Perhaps she knows something?"

Claveston grabbed the lad's skinny arms and gave them a squeeze. "By King George, lad, I hope you're right, or poor Miss Lefebvre is in dire trouble."

He hurried back up to the house, entering the servants' domain by the back door. Bonnet was in his office, and jumped to his feet as Claveston barged in. "Jeanie Green," he demanded. "Where will I find her now?"

"She'll be up cleaning the West Wing, your sister's rooms I believe," the butler said, without needing to check a rota. There was little that happened in this house without him knowing. He had been extremely helpful in arranging for each member of staff to see him in the past couple of days, though Claveston knew how much the thought that Bonnet had somehow failed the family must be burning the elderly butler up inside - and Claveston knew that Bonnet was furious that something had been stolen out from under his patrician nose, without his knowing anything about it.

"Thank you," Claveston said as he raced along the corridor and made his way up the back stairs. He took them two at a time, in his haste, all the way to the second floor. He burst into the corridor. It was empty. He walked along it briskly, for once not noticing the eyes of the paintings of his ancestors as they stared down at him. He turned the corner into the West Wing and was surprised to see his sister and one of the maids talking in whispers.

Miss Lefebvre's words came back to him. "Per'aps fifteen, maybe twenty minutes," she had said was the time it had taken his sister to go and fetch ribbons from her rooms. It took no more than ten, even if she had been forced to search for them a little. He realized that he hadn't asked Miss Lefebvre if his sister had returned with the ribbons in question.

He waited until the young maid and his sister had finished their clandestine conversation, and for Gertrude to go into her rooms before he made his way back to Miss Lefebvre's chambers. He barged in without knocking. She jumped up from her desk, her eyes wide. "Lord Wycliffe!"

"This will not take a moment. Did Gertrude actually bring the ribbons downstairs with her?" Miss Lefebvre looked at him blankly. "You said that she went upstairs to fetch ribbons she wished to sew onto her gown. Did she bring them with her to the music room?"

"No, I assumed she 'ad put them in the drawing-room, so she could do her sewing once her lesson was over," Miss Lefebvre said, looking very confused.

Claveston stormed out of her rooms and flung every door open wide as he searched for Jeanie Green. He found her in Gertrude's old nursery, polishing the brasses in the fireplace. The girl jumped to her feet and bobbed a curtsey respectfully as he entered the room. She was no more than fifteen, the same age as his sister. She kept her eyes lowered, she was shy and timid, and looked petrified to see him.

Just seeing her so afraid made his anger dissipate immediately. He felt sorry for this poor girl. "Don't worry," he assured her. "I just want the truth."

Her face was pale, and her hands shook as she answered his questions. "Did my sister ask you to do something for her?" he asked gently. She nodded. Poor mite, it was clear she'd somehow gotten caught up in something she wanted no part of – especially now. "Did she ask you to fetch something for her?"

"Yes, my Lord," the girl said so quietly that Claveston could barely hear her. "She said her mother asked her to fetch the tiara from her rooms, as it needed cleanin'. She said she couldn't do it 'erself as she had to go to her music lesson, and that if I left it in her chamber, she would be sure 'n see it was sent out as her mother wanted when she was done."

"You've not been with us long, have you?" Claveston asked the poor girl.

She shook her head. "No, my Lord. Just four months." She looked up at him, her eyes full of fear. "Please don't turn me out, my Lord. Me Ma's just had another littl'un, and they need me wages," she pleaded.

"I can't guarantee how my father will feel about all this, but I am inclined to believe that you did not know you were doing anything untoward. I will do what I can for you, but you need to prepare yourself for the worst. If he lets you go, I'll give you a character, even if he won't and I'll see if I can get you placed somewhere. I promise."

Leaving the poor maid standing, tears pouring down her pale cheeks, Claveston strode towards his sister's rooms.

There was nobody there. He peered around the dressing room door, and into her bed-chamber, but there was no sign of his sister. He hurried downstairs and looked in the drawing-room, then the music room, the library, and then went outside onto the terrace. He glanced over the gardens, finally seeing his sister, walking nonchalantly through the knot garden. He raced towards her, fury raging inside him.

"Gertrude," he shouted as he drew closer. "Where is the dress that you sewed ribbons onto that day?"

"What dress?" Gertrude asked, looking genuinely bewildered. She picked a sprig of lavender and lifted it to her nose. She took a deep breath and sighed contentedly. Claveston could hardly believe how little she seemed to care about what she had done.

"You were late for your music lesson that day, weren't you?"

Gertrude paused, blinking rapidly, her mouth agape. "I don't know. I might have been."

"You were. You said you had to fetch some ribbons to sew onto a dress."

"Then that is probably what happened," Gertrude said, her eyes wide. She was doing a good job of feigning innocence, but Claveston knew her too well – and God forgive him, but he believed both Miss Lefebvre and Jeanie Green more than he did his own sister right now.

He had heard the quaver in Gertrude's voice and could see the fear in her eyes.

"If I go to the drawing-room, will I find any ribbons in your sewing box?" he asked her. "And if I ask Mrs. Grint to go through your gowns, will we find one with newly added ribbons?"

"Claveston, you are being ridiculous," Gertrude said, laughing nervously.

"Am I? Or are you the only person I didn't think I needed to question? I presumed that your affections for Miss Lefebvre were genuine, that you would never wish to do anything to hurt her."

"Are you accusing me of having taken Mama's tiara?"

"No," Claveston said firmly. "I think – no, I know that you got someone else to take the tiara, and you just placed it in Miss Lefebvre's rooms. I think you thought that if anyone other than your companion was found guilty, then you could absolve yourself of all blame as you didn't actually take it yourself. I think that if I call Jeanie Green here now and ask her what happened, that she will tell me everything – just as she did a few moments ago."

"There's nothing to tell," Gertrude said brazenly. "Call her in. Question her. She won't tell you that's what happened, as it is ridiculous. And I cannot believe that you would believe the tattle of a servant over your own sister." She was more defensive now, like a cornered animal. "Why would I do such a thing?" she asked, her tone desperate, frantic almost. "I love Sophie. I would never wish her to leave. Without her, I will have no Season at all – as there will be nobody to accompany me."

Claveston had to agree that she had half a point. But something wasn't right. He knew that Gertrude had arranged for Jeanie to take the tiara. Gertrude knew that he knew the truth, so why was she still denying it?

He wanted to help. He wanted to understand why. Gertrude was clearly angry at someone. Perhaps she had finally started to turn her frustrations upon those who deserved them, their parents. By stealing Mama's tiara, Mama had been forced to stay longer. Maybe that had been Gertrude's plan all along, maybe she had never intended for Sophie to be blamed. Perhaps everything had just gone wrong. But none of it made any sense.

"Go to your rooms. I will be back to speak with you again, later, young lady," he warned her.

Gertrude simply laughed. "You are not my Papa," she said hurtfully. "You don't have the right to tell me what to do."

Her words still stinging his ears, Claveston watched his sister as she did as she was told – for once – and went back inside. Within just a few moments, he saw her sad face at her window. He hung his head and prayed for guidance. How had things come to this?

The sound of a carriage on the driveway alerted Claveston to the passing of time. The three days were nearly over. Tonight, he would have to be able to explain to his father precisely what had happened, or Miss Lefebvre would be put out of the house – or worse. Yet how could he possibly tell his parents that the theft had been undertaken on Gertrude's behalf? How would he ever explain that to his parents when he did not fully understand it himself?

Peering out of the window, Claveston was surprised to see that Cormick had returned. Normally he would be delighted to receive an unexpected visit from his dear friend, but today it seemed to be a distraction he did not need right now. He watched as his friend bounced out of the carriage with his usual vigor, smiling at everyone nearby. Despite his lack of time, Claveston's heart lifted just at the sight of the man. He gave a wry chuckle. Perhaps providence had sent Cormick to him. He needed help with all of this, and here was one of the finest men he knew.

Making his way downstairs, he heard his father announce to Bonnet that he would be in his study until dinner, that he wasn't to be disturbed. Claveston couldn't help but be grateful for such a reprieve. It would give him time to plan what to say when the inevitable discussion about Miss Lefebvre's future actually occurred.

Cormick greeted him with a firm handshake and a good-natured slap on the back. "You look like death, my friend," he said. "Have things been so bad?"

"No, I think they may be worse."

"Tell me everything, but first call for some lemonade and cake. I'm famished after the trip," Cormick said with a wink. Claveston chuckled. His friend's appetite was almost legendary. He called for Mrs. Grint, who beamed when she saw Cormick and knew without even being asked what he required.

CHAPTER FOURTEEN

The two young men went into Claveston's favored drawing-room and sank into chairs by the fire. "So, tell me what has you in such a snit?" Cormick said as he crossed his long legs and relaxed back into the wing-back chair.

"I don't even know where to begin," Claveston admitted. "It has been the most terrible few days." He paused and took a deep breath. "Miss Lefebvre has been accused of theft."

"You cannot be serious," Cormick said, his expression aghast at such a thought. "She is such a decent, upright, honest sort."

"Yes, she is," Claveston agreed as Mrs. Grint appeared with a tray of delicious treats and a large jug of lemonade for Cormick – who seemed to even barely notice her arrival, so keen was he to hear the details. "A tiara was found in her armoire; a very expensive tiara that my grandmother wore for her presentation at court. One my mother also wore, and one that Gertrude will wear very soon for hers."

"I cannot believe that Miss Lefebvre would take such a thing."

"Neither could I," Claveston admitted, pouring a glass of lemonade for his guest and another for himself. He took a couple of gulps to try and moisten his dry mouth and sighed heavily. "My father gave me three days to get to the bottom of the matter and to find proof that Miss Lefebvre did not do it, before he puts her out – or, worse, in front of the magistrate."

"You cannot let such a thing happen. She is a good woman. She does not deserve such a thing."

"I am well aware of that," Claveston snapped. "And I have the evidence to clear her name."

"Then why the long face?" Cormick reached for a slice of cake and took a bite. He chewed a couple of times then stopped. He swallowed hurriedly. "Oh my, the truth of what happened is as bad as the thought of Miss Lefebvre being responsible?"

"Exactly that," Claveston said sadly. "I learned that Gertrude is to blame."

"Ahh," Cormick said and exhaled loudly. "I cannot say I am entirely surprised by such a turn of events."

"You aren't?" Claveston was stunned by his friend's reaction. He had expected shock, dismay – yet Cormick was showing neither of those things. He simply looked sad.

"I am sure that in her mind, that Lady Gertrude simply wished to cause a little trouble for Miss Lefebvre. I cannot imagine that she would ever wish to have her companion put out of the house, and most certainly would not wish her to risk facing the gallows."

"But?" Claveston queried. "Gertrude is not a fool. She must have known the consequences of her actions, Cormick? I cannot believe that she wished Miss Lefebvre harm, yet what she has done could only ever lead to that. What possible reason could she have? I truly believed that she liked her companion."

"Young girls are a peculiar breed, indeed," Cormick said sagely. "And Lady Gertrude is used to being the very center of your world. You must confess that since Miss Lefebvre's arrival here at Compton, that might not entirely be the case any longer. Lady Gertrude is very alert, she sees everything that goes on around her. Is it not possible that she felt set aside?"

"You think she did this out of jealousy?" It was a plausible explanation, yet Claveston could not think Gertrude so petty. She was still young, and her emotions were still volatile, but she was not unkind. If she had wanted to rid herself of her companion, all she would have needed to do was to say so to Mama, or to Papa. They had ever indulged her and had got rid of countless nannies and governesses for no reason other than that Gertrude did not like them over the years.

"I do," Cormick said. "If she has seen what I have, then she has seen someone come into her home and, without intention, do something no other woman has ever done before."

"Which is?"

"Win your heart," Cormick said simply. "Miss

Lefebvre is the biggest threat to her position in your heart, and she fears losing her place there."

"That does not excuse her actions," Claveston said, aggrieved. If that was Gertrude's reason, then it made him partly to blame. He had done all he could to make Gertrude feel safe and loved, since she was tiny, to make up for the lack of their parents' affections. He had placed her at the very center of his life. He did all he could to ensure her happiness. He could not see how Gertrude could ever think that anyone would ever usurp her in his heart. Yet he had to be permitted to find love for himself, too.

"No, it does not. But it might explain them. Jealousy can make us do peculiar things. I don't know if she wished to punish you or Miss Lefebvre – perhaps it was both of you – but her hurt may have forced her to lash out."

The two men sat in silence for a few moments. Claveston lost in his thoughts, Cormick intent upon devouring everything upon the tray that Mrs. Grint had brought up for him. Cormick's explanation might well be closer to the truth than perhaps Gertrude herself realized. She had done a terrible thing, but she had done it because of the hurt that had been her constant companion. Not only was Miss Lefebvre someone Claveston cared for deeply, but she was also someone Gertrude had grown close to. He had never seen his sister open up to someone the way she had to Miss Lefebvre. Perhaps the thought that he might take Miss Lefebvre from her, as well as the thought that Miss Lefebvre might have taken her spot in Claveston's heart made it doubly hard for her to bear?

Whatever her reasons, Gertrude needed his love and support – and he would have to talk with her. She had to confess to Papa what she had done. It was not right that an innocent woman's life is ruined by her petty jealousies. He did not doubt that he was the last person she would want to speak to, after their confrontation earlier, but she had to know that even if he loved Miss Lefebvre, even if he was lucky enough to be permitted to marry her – if Miss Lefebvre would even consider him after all that had occurred this week - that such a thing would never change the way he felt about Gertrude.

~

Sophie was going out of her mind as she waited for news. Being confined to her rooms was frustrating. She had too much time to think and wonder why anyone would do such a thing. Since Claveston's visit, she had pondered Gertrude's tardiness that fateful day. There had been more than enough time for the young woman to fetch her ribbons and take them to the drawing-room. Yet she could not think why Gertrude could possibly want to hurt her in such a dreadful way.

She had almost finished her packing. She knew all too well that whatever the outcome of Lord Wycliffe's investigations that she would be leaving this house tonight. She was tempted to call for the carriage, to leave now rather than wait to have her fate decided for her. But she knew that she needed to see this through, to be brave and face up to whatever might be.

She opened the doors of her armoire and began to

pull out her gowns to lay them on the bed. She had left this part of her packing until last, because the armoire was where the tiara had been found. She felt as if everything inside it had been soiled by the presence of the stolen tiara. She vowed to wash every item as soon as she found somewhere to stay.

Normally she would roll each gown in velvet carefully, to prevent creasing during her travels, but today she took much less care. She folded everything and crammed it into her trunk, leaving behind all of the new gowns that the duchess had insisted her dressmaker make up for Sophie. She would not take a thing that she had not paid for herself.

A timid knock on her door made Sophie glance up. She called out that whoever it was should enter, but the door did not open. She shook her head and assumed that perhaps she had just misheard, maybe a bird had just flown into the window or a breeze had made the door rattle a little. But a few moments later, there was another knock.

Sophie got up and moved to the door. She opened it and was surprised to see a shamefaced Gertrude stood before her. "Lady Gertrude," Sophie said softly. "Would you like to come in?"

Gertrude bit at her lip and fidgeted from one foot to the other. "I...I'm sorry," she said, then burst into tears.

Sophie sighed heavily, put her arm around the girl, and took her inside her room. She sat Gertrude down and gave her a glass of water and a clean handkerchief. Gertrude wiped her eyes and blew her nose, loudly, then took a sip of the water. "I truly am sorry. I never meant for things to go this far," she said earnestly.

"I am sure you didn't," Sophie said softly, trying hard to maintain her composure. Gertrude was just a child in so many ways. She had never had to face up to the consequences of her actions, everything had been given to her before she'd even asked. She was spoilt in every way – except for the one thing she needed the most, unconditional love.

"I was so angry," Gertrude said desperately. "I don't know which I feared most, losing you – or losing Claveston."

"I don't know what you mean," Sophie said, perplexed by such a statement. "Why would you lose either one of us?"

"Because it is clear to anyone with eyes that he loves you. He flirts with you and pays you attention he used to pay to me. He seeks you out. He only spends time with me, because by doing so he can be with you," Gertrude wailed.

Sophie shook her head. "Your brother loves you, how can you doubt it? He has done all in his power to ensure that he is there for you. He gives you time he does not 'ave, every single day so you will not feel this way."

"Not since you came," Gertrude protested. "It has been different. I know it has. He is there with me, yet he looks to you for your approval at every turn. He seeks your opinion, rather than mine – and the way he looks upon you." She sighed. "He dotes upon you, hangs on your every word."

"I do not think he does," Sophie said, "but if you are

right, it does not change anything. He is still your brother, and he loves you. He will always love you and be there for you. I am simply a member of the 'ousehold staff. There can never be anything more than that between us."

"You do not know Claveston if you think that," Gertrude said with a sad smile. "Once he knows what he wants, he always gets it."

"That is as maybe, but that assumes that I would want the same thing," Sophie said, feeling uncomfortable at the turn this conversation had taken. "I told you when I first came here that your brother would not be the kind of man I would ever see in that way."

"But that has changed, you cannot deny it," Gertrude said perceptively. "I see it in your eyes. You care for him."

Sophie did not know how to respond. The girl was right. Her feelings for Lord Wycliffe had changed since she'd told Gertrude that she wouldn't leave her and that she had no designs to ensnare Lord Wycliffe in marriage. She still had no intention of trying to entrap him, but she did love him. "Gertrude, even if we did both love one another, as you believe, there is nothing that can come of that."

"I know, which would mean that you would probably leave – and you promised that you would not leave me."

"So, you came up with a scheme that was bound only to end in my banishment?"

Gertrude started crying again, great hiccupping sobs. "I did not think it through," she said. "I just wanted to punish you both for breaking your promises to me. But it went so wrong. I never meant for you to be sent away. I just wanted to tarnish you in Claveston's eyes. I should have known better."

"Oh, Gertrude," Sophie said, putting an arm around the girl's shoulders and pulling her close. "You are such a child. There has been so much pressure put upon you these past months, with the preparations for your debut. But you must learn to think before you act. This could have not only lost me my position but my life."

"I know that now," Gertrude cried. "I am so sorry. I truly did not think there would be anything like this. I didn't know. I didn't. I would not want to see anyone hung for something I did. And Claveston knows, and he will tell them that it was me and I cannot bear that he thinks me so cruel."

"Then you must tell your parents before they find out from someone else. Prove to them, to Claveston, how grown-up you can be. Show how contrite you are, as you 'ave done to me."

"But they will punish me. Can you not tell them for me?"

Sophie laughed. She had not meant to but could not contain it. "They will not listen to me now, Gertrude," she reminded the girl. "I doubt they'd even see me if I asked for an audience."

Gertrude stared at her with wide eyes. Sophie had the strangest feeling that though she had realized that what she had done was wrong and some of the harm that her actions had caused, Gertrude had only just seen that she had lost both of her champions. Her actions had brought about what she had feared the most.

If Claveston did indeed know what she had done,

then he would be torn right now. He would wish to save both Sophie and his sister, but Gertrude obviously feared that he would choose Sophie. And given what she had done to Sophie, she would no longer be in a position to intervene on her charge's behalf. Nobody would listen to a woman charged with being a thief.

CHAPTER FIFTEEN

Claveston went to his sister's rooms, only to find them empty. He punched the door, furious that she had ignored his order to stay there until he returned. He was shocked when he went out into the corridor to see her emerging, red-eyed from Miss Lefebvre's chambers. She turned her head and saw him. Her eyes were wide with fear. "Please don't shout at me," she begged. "I'm going to see Papa. I'm going to tell him that it was all my fault."

Claveston was surprised at her words, but he was also proud of her. "Miss Lefebvre convinced you to tell the truth?"

"Not exactly," Gertrude admitted shamefacedly. "After you knew, I went to her and confessed. I never meant for things to go so far - you have to believe that. I didn't know how Mama and Papa would react so angrily. It all got out of hand so quickly."

Claveston shook his head. How could she possibly have known how their parents would react to such a thing. She barely knew them. They'd been around so little, and all she'd ever seen of them was their generous and lazy affection. She knew so little of the real world, and he blamed himself for that. He could have done more for her, to teach her how hard life could be for those born without their privileges. But as her brother, that should not have been his role. Such teaching should have come from loving parents.

"I will come with you," he said supportively. "I think it is time we told Mama and Papa that their actions are as much to blame as anything else."

They made their way down the stairs, arm in arm. Claveston could feel his sister was shaking violently. She was so scared of what might happen. "I love you," he whispered as they stopped for a moment outside Papa's office. "And I am proud of you."

She gave him a wan smile and raised her tiny fist to rap on the door. The knock was timid, but Papa obviously still heard it. "Enter," he barked loudly.

Claveston pressed a kiss to Gertrude's forehead and gave her a quick squeeze. She laid her hand on the doorknob and turned it, opening the door cautiously and stepping inside. She turned back to her brother. "I think I should do this alone," she said bravely and shut him outside.

Claveston pressed his ear to the door. At first, the voices were so quiet he could barely make out a thing, but his father's voice grew louder and soon Gertrude was shouting just as loud as him, just in order to be heard. A few moments later the door was flung open. Claveston jumped back out of his father's way. Papa stomped up the stairs and was soon out of sight.

Claveston peered around the study door. Gertrude was sitting in front of Papa's desk, her head in her hands, sobbing loudly. Claveston hurried to her side and hugged her tightly. "You did the right thing," he assured her, kissing her cheek and rubbing her back as she cried into his shoulder.

"Will he still put Sophie out?" Gertrude whispered.

"I don't know, but I doubt she'll stay even if he doesn't. Would you wish to stay somewhere when you'd been accused of theft?"

Gertrude shook her pretty head. "No, I suppose I wouldn't. And so, I will lose the only friend I've ever really had, and it is all my own fault."

There was nothing that Claveston could say to that. He was sure that Sophie would go. He would not wish to stay somewhere that had put him through such an ordeal. The voices of his parents in the hallway made him stand up and wander towards the door.

"We have wronged her," Papa was saying to Mama as they drew near. "I can hardly believe a child of ours would create such a fiction and cause such great harm."

"She should stay if she wishes to do so. But something needs to be done about the child," Mama said dismissively as if she didn't care much one way or the other.

Their conversation riled Claveston. "Do you not wonder why she might do such a thing?"

"Because she is spoiled and thinks there are no consequences to such actions," Mama said, looking put out by it all.

"And why is she that way?" Claveston asked. "Or do you not think that far?"

"Be careful," Papa said sternly. "Remember your place, my boy."

"And where is my place?" Claveston asked angrily. "Is it doing precisely as I am told, with no real purpose in life other than that you deem to give me? Is it as my sister's parent, as her parents are never here to actually act in that place? Is it to run the household that neither of you care enough for to actually spend more than a few weeks a year in?"

"You overstep," Papa roared. "How dare you speak to us in such a way."

"How dare I? How dare I?" Claveston asked incredulously. "You have done nothing to raise either myself or Gertrude. Mama has made it clear that even being present for her daughter's most important Season, her very first, is not important enough for her to be present throughout its entirety. I was bundled off to school and expected to raise myself, while Gertrude has seen a parade of nannies and governesses come and go. Yet despite never doing anything to deserve our love and respect, you demand it whenever you deign to breeze into our lives."

"Such nonsense," Mama said dismissively. "Your lives are no different to any other child of our acquaintance."

"Now that is simply not true," Claveston retorted. "I have had more loving care and support from Cormick's family than from my own. Mrs. Grint has been more of a mother to us than you have been, with all your trips abroad to find yet another trinket we don't need."

"How dare you," Mama said, her eyes wide now. "I have done everything I can to ensure you have all you need and want."

"All we ever wanted was you," Gertrude said sadly as she emerged from the study. "Why can you never see that?"

Nobody said anything. What was there to be said? Gertrude had said everything that needed to be said. Claveston could see the pain in his sister's eyes and heard every bit of longing she had in her voice – a longing that was echoed in his own heart.

He put an arm around her waist and escorted her up to her rooms. She crawled into her bed, fully dressed, and curled up into a tight ball. "Everything will be alright," he tried to assure her.

"No, it won't," she said. "Sophie will leave, whether Mama and Papa dismiss her or not. They will leave, again. At some point, you will go back to London and I will be here alone. Nothing ever changes."

There was nothing Claveston could say to that, either. He kissed her tenderly and left her to cry and to sleep. He made his way back downstairs. His parents were huddled together in his father's study. They no longer looked angry and shocked. But they also did not look happy. Clearly words had continued to be exchanged after he and Gertrude had left. He wondered precisely what it was that the couple had been arguing over.

His father beckoned him inside. "Your mother and I have been discussing our plans for the next few months," he said briskly. "I think we can ensure that one or other of us is here and that we are both here together more often."

"Gertrude will be glad of that," Claveston said softly. It was too late for him, but perhaps it wasn't for Gertrude.

"I will ensure I am here for the entirety of Gertrude's Season," Mama said. "You are right, I should be there."

"And I shall make sure I am in London for her presentation at Court and will throw her a grand ball," Papa said.

"She doesn't need a grand ball," Claveston said. "She just needs you there, at least from time to time."

They both nodded. "And Miss Lefebvre. She needs her, does she not?" Mama asked.

"I believe so, but I doubt if she will wish to remain part of this household after all she has gone through," Claveston said sadly.

"Do you think there is any way you can convince her to remain?" Papa asked.

Claveston thought for a moment before he responded. There was a way he longed for Sophie to stay, but despite all that Cormick had said, he wasn't sure if his feelings for her were reciprocated. "I don't know," he said simply.

"Will you try and talk to her?" Papa asked.

"I think it might be best if the two of you do. You need to apologize for all you've put her through. I doubt she'll stay without that, so you may as well try that first."

~

FROM TIME TO TIME, Sophie could hear raised voices coming from downstairs. She couldn't make out what they were saying, but it seemed as if the family was fracturing around her. She couldn't help feeling guilty, even though she knew that the family had been fragile long before her arrival – and that it was Gertrude's actions that had brought them to this point.

She continued to pack her things and was just closing her trunk when there was a knock on her door. She was stunned to see the Duke and Duchess of Compton hovering in the hallway. They both looked nervous, something she'd not ever seen in either of them before. "May we come in?" they asked politely.

"It is your house, you may go wherever you wish," Sophie said quietly as she stood back to let them in.

The duchess took a seat on the sofa in Sophie's small parlor. The duke stood before the fireplace his hands folded behind his back. Sophie stood quietly by the door, waiting to hear what they had come to say. It was strange to see them together in the same room, especially one as small as this. "We must offer you our sincerest apologies," the duchess said, her expression grave. "We have wronged you, and we now know exactly what has happened."

"Thank you, your Grace," Sophie said generously.

The duke glanced around the room. His eyes rested on the trunk a few feet away from where Sophie was stood. "You are already packed?" he asked then looked a little sheepish for stating the obvious.

"I assumed that whatever 'appened that you would not wish me to remain here," Sophie said simply.

"We do not wish you to go," the duchess said. "But we do understand if you think you have no other choice."

"Would you stay, if you were me, your Grace?" Sophie asked.

"No," the duke admitted. "I would never wish to see any of us ever again."

"And a part of me feels that way, your Grace," Sophie admitted. "Your lack of trust in me has hurt me terribly."

"I don't doubt it," the duchess said. "And for that we are truly sorry. And I know Gertrude is sorry, too."

"As do I," Sophie said. "She spoke to me before she came to you."

"She needs you," the duke said.

"If I might speak frankly?" Sophie asked. They both nodded. "She does not. She needs the two of you."

"Our son has already pointed that out to us," the duchess said drily. "You are right of course, but she needs you, too."

"I would like to see her Coming Out. I believe she has learned much since I 'ave arrived, and I would like to see 'ow well she applies it. But I am not sure if I want that enough to forget what 'as happened in the past few days."

"We understand," the duke said. "Take your time to think it over. Do not leave right away. There is no rush for you to make up your mind, but know that you are wanted, you are trusted, and you are needed here."

They departed, leaving Sophie alone with her thoughts. She looked out of the window and saw Mr. Cormick wandering through the gardens. He had proven himself a good listener in the past, and she was glad he was here visiting at a time when she could use an understanding ear. She reached for her wrap and headed outside, hurrying to where she had last seen him. She found him wandering in the kitchen garden, talking to one of the gardeners.

"Miss Lefebvre, how delightful to see you," he said, bowing deeply. His smile was warm, and she found herself smiling back at him, despite the pit of misery deep inside her.

"I cannot tell you 'ow 'appy I am to see you," she said as she gave him a respectful curtsey. He offered her his arm, which she took gladly. They walked along the gravel paths and he pointed out some of the crops that would soon be on the table. She was surprised he knew so much about such things, but it was clear that he was an unusual man.

"So, I understand that your name has been cleared," Mr. Cormick said politely as they entered the formal gardens, out of earshot of the gardeners.

"It 'as, and though I expected to be leaving this evening, I 'ave been asked to remain in my position."

"And you are hesitant?"

"I am," she admitted. "I 'ave been badly let down by Lady Gertrude. What she did 'as hurt me deeply, though I understand why she did it. I do not feel safe here. Yet I do not 'ave anywhere else to go, so am loathe to walk away from a position until I 'ave a new one."

"And despite it all, you are fond of Lady Gertrude and Lord Claveston, am I right?"

She nodded. "I am. My 'eart and my 'ead are in a terrible muddle."

"Would it help if I told you that he loves you?" Mr.

Cormick asked, a twinkle in his eye. Sophie stared at him, her mouth agape.

"I do not think so, Mr. Cormick."

"Do you not? Oh, I do. In fact, I know so, because he told me."

CHAPTER SIXTEEN

Sophie stayed. Not because both Mrs. Grint and Mr. Cormick had told her that Lord Wycliffe loved her, but because she had promised Gertrude that she would not leave her. Despite everything that had happened, Sophie discovered that her promise to the girl was a powerful thing. Gertrude needed to learn that some people did keep their promises. That they didn't turn away, even when things were hard.

In truth, that she had learned of Lord Wycliffe's feelings only made things harder. Seeing him every single day, knowing that she had feelings for him and that he had feelings for her that they could never act upon was torment. But things had changed at Compton. The duchess did not go on her trip. She actually let her agent act in her stead, and together she and Sophie did all they could to prepare Gertrude for the Season. They never spoke of what had happened again, but from time-to-time Sophie caught the duchess looking at her, her eyes soft and sad. She knew the duchess felt guilty, but Sophie had forgiven her.

They would leave for London in just two days' time, and the house was caught in a flurry of activity as trunks were packed and essential household items were sent on ahead of the family. Claveston visited the schoolroom often, helping Sophie to demonstrate dances for Gertrude, and singing as Gertrude played so she had a wide repertoire of pieces she could play at soirees in town.

Gertrude was quiet and deferential to both Sophie and her mother. She seemed quite changed by her experience. She apologized to Sophie every day, numerous times a day, and Sophie told her over and over that she did not need to do so, that she was quite forgiven. She hoped that Gertrude would one day know that Sophie truly meant it.

"Mama," Claveston said, bursting into the drawing room. "Oh, I'm sorry, Miss Lefebvre, I did not know you were here."

"Your mother is in the orangerie," Sophie said with a smile. She had not seen much of Claveston recently. His father had kept him busy, teaching him more about the family's investments, and giving him more real responsibility for a number of them. He looked well, his eyes bright, though his clothing was more sedate than his usual style. He wore a plain black coat, with a matching waistcoat and a cream shirt and cravat, making him seem somehow more serious and grown-up than he ever had before.

"How have you been, Miss Lefebvre?" he asked her, hovering in the doorway, not coming any closer.

"I 'ave been well," she admitted.

"And things have been good here?" He looked concerned on her behalf.

"They 'ave. Everyone seems determined to make it up to me," she said with a smile.

"I am glad," he said softly.

"Thank you for all you did to clear my name."

"Thank you for staying. I think we all need you more than we would ever dare to admit."

With that, he disappeared. Sophie hugged his words to her heart. She knew nothing could ever come of her feelings for him, but Lord Wycliffe had captured her heart, unexpectedly and completely. She sometimes wished he had not, that she still thought him the selfish dandy she had first experienced. Life would be so much easier that way.

The rest of her day was filled with packing and other duties, and she didn't have time to think about him again until she was getting ready for dinner. She dressed carefully, choosing her favorite wine-red velvet gown. She took extra care curling her hair and applied just a touch of rouge to her cheeks and lips before going downstairs.

The family was gathered in the library, one of the only rooms not in disarray due to the upcoming move to the London house. Gertrude looked lovely, her hair curled becomingly, framing her pretty face. She wore a gown with a delicate floral pattern that made her look girlish, yet sophisticated. She would break many hearts in London, of that Sophie had no doubt.

The duke beamed when she entered the room and brought her a small glass of ratafia as she entered. "You look lovely," he said to her. "That color goes so well with your lovely green eyes."

"Thank you, your Grace," Sophie said, bobbing him a curtsey.

Gertrude hurried forwards and tucked her arm through Sophie's. "I am so happy. I can hardly believe that we leave for London so soon. And that you are still by my side."

The duchess beamed at her, and Claveston bowed. Sophie felt her cheeks flush. It seemed that every eye was on her and nobody seemed to wish to say anything, though their eyes were all bright with amusement. Sophie did not enjoy being on the outside of whatever it was that was amusing them all so much, but she did not have long to wait until she found out what it was. The gong for dinner sounded and the duke offered her his arm and escorted her to the dining room. Following just behind them, Claveston escorted his mother and sister. Bonnet opened the doors, and Sophie gasped.

Around the table stood Lord William and Lady Mary, Lady Charlotte and Captain James, and even Anne Knorr, Lady Mary's former companion. "Happy birthday," they chorused, all at once.

Sophie felt tears prick at her eyes and raised her hands to her cover her mouth in an attempt to hide her surprise and delight. In moments, she was being embraced by dear Charlotte, then Lady Mary. Lord William and Captain James bowed to her and beamed, and Miss Knorr grinned, obviously delighted to have been included in the surprise. "Was this you?" Sophie said, turning to Gertrude.

"No, I did not even know it was your birthday until yesterday when Claveston told me about this evening's entertainments," she admitted. "He did not dare tell me earlier, in case I gave the surprise away."

Lord Wycliffe was blushing when Sophie turned to thank him. She didn't know what to say. After all that had happened, to see her dear friends meant more to her than he could ever know. He nodded at her, as if he understood exactly what she was thinking. She hoped he knew just how much this meant to her.

She wiped her eyes and took her seat next to Charlotte. Conversation around the table was the most enjoyable that Sophie could remember. Everyone seemed delighted to be there. Jokes were made and stories told. From time to time, Charlotte reached over and took Sophie's hand, giving it a little squeeze and smiling at her.

After the meal, the women got up and went into the drawing-room, leaving the men to their port and cigars. Charlotte and Sophie took a moment out on the terrace to speak alone. "Are you quite well?" Charlotte asked her, her eyes full of concern. "When you wrote to us of what happened, I wanted to come to your rescue. James had to stop me."

"I am quite well. Things are better than ever," Sophie admitted. "The family is trying so hard to be a family now."

"I am glad. Sometimes it is the strangest things that make everything work, is it not?"

"I cannot disagree. I would have preferred it if things

'ad not been so difficult," Sophie said with a wry smile, "but I think all is behind us now."

"And Claveston is in love with you," Charlotte noted perceptively.

"I don't think so. Others keep telling me so, but he 'as never given me the slightest inclination of such feelings," Sophie said, a little sadly.

"Oh, and you love him," Charlotte said. "I wasn't sure until just now. But you do, don't you?"

Sophie knew that she could not deny it, not to Charlotte. "I do. But it is for nothing, as he cannot marry someone like me."

"I do not see why not," Charlotte said briskly. "You are the daughter of a baron, and one who has sufficient money to provide an excellent dowry for you. You are more of a catch than you think yourself."

"I am old. Nobody will take a woman my age to wife."

"I am the same age as you," Charlotte reminded her. "James took me."

"That is different, and you well know it," Sophie said. "Why?"

"Because you already 'ad a child, so 'ad proof of your fertility," Sophie said impatiently. "And, because he 'ad loved you from when you were a girl. It is not the same."

"Love is the same. And I doubt if Claveston has even once thought about your fertility. He just knows what he wants. And he tends to get what he wants," Charlotte reminded her patiently.

"So why does he never say anything to me?" Sophie

asked. "If he wants me so badly, why does he not do anything about it?"

⌖

"Mostly because I am an idiot," Claveston said as he emerged from the French doors onto the terrace, a rueful smile on his lips. Charlotte grinned, hugged Miss Lefebvre, and moved far enough away that she could say she had acted as a chaperone to them, but also so that they might speak in private.

"My lord," she said shyly. "You shouldn't speak that way."

"No, it is true. I should have told you months ago that the reason I wanted you to act as Gertrude's companion was because I adored you. But I was a fool. I brought you here and kept that to myself."

Miss Lefebvre stared at him, her eyes wide. She did not know how to respond to him, and now he'd admitted it out loud, Claveston had no idea what to say either. He looked down into her emerald eyes and wondered what she was thinking. She was so hard to read. He had only overheard a small part of her conversation with Lady Charlotte, but he was sure that this was the moment he had to tell her everything. His greatest fear was that some good-looking, sensible, caring man might notice her in London, propose and he would lose her forever.

"You brought my friends here, thank you for that," Miss Lefebvre said awkwardly, breaking what had become a somewhat awkward silence. She was wringing her hands and seemed as uncomfortable as he felt.

"It was my pleasure," he said with a gentle smile. She was so easily pleased. He marveled that he had gotten so much so wrong when she'd first arrived. "I hope you can see that I listened and that I heard you when you told me what you wanted."

She gave him a perplexed look. "I don't understand."

"When I arranged that ridiculous party, afterward you said that you preferred more intimate events, like a supper with good friends."

"Ah," Miss Lefebvre said with a shy smile. "And you remembered my birthday, I don't remember ever telling you of it?"

"You did not. I asked Lady Charlotte," he admitted. "I've been planning this for weeks. I wanted you to know how much you are appreciated here, especially after everything that happened."

"Thank you," Miss Lefebvre said. "It has been a wonderful evening."

"I am glad you are enjoying it," Claveston said, wondering how she would react if he reached out and caressed her cheek. She was looking up at him with such tenderness in her eyes. Tentatively he reached out. She leaned into his hand and closed her eyes. Claveston bit at his lip, unsure of himself and what he should do next.

Suddenly, Miss Lefebvre pulled away from him, looking guilty. "We should go inside," she said stepping away. Impulsively, Claveston reached out and grabbed her wrist, pulling her back towards him. He pressed a tender kiss to her lips. Her eyes pinged wide but then closed as she kissed him back.

"Ahem," Lady Charlotte coughed behind them.

They jumped apart and stared at one another as if they had never seen each other before. Miss Lefebvre raised her fingers to her lips, as if she could still feel his lips there – as he could sense hers. "If I were to speak to my father, would you give me permission to write to yours?" he asked her, taking her hand in his and pressing a kiss to the inside of her wrist, an intimate and tender caress he hoped would tell her his intentions were honorable, but also passionate.

She flushed from her chest to the tips of her ears and nodded, speechless. Then she yanked her hand away from his and ran from him. Charlotte gave him an unreadable look, then followed her friend into the night. Claveston wasn't sure if things had gone well or not, but he had her permission to ask his father for permission to marry. He would do so as soon as he could. He did not want to go to London without being affianced to Sophie Lefebvre.

He went inside. His mother and father were talking quietly together in one corner of the room, while his sister and Miss Knorr were chatting animatedly on the sofa with Lady Mary. He hadn't noticed it earlier, but from the swell of her belly, his friend was about to become a father. Claveston smiled and joined his friends where they stood at the fireplace.

"So, you have kept that news quiet," he said, nodding towards Mary. William chuckled. "She is quite well? I know she has had her troubles with her health."

"She is the healthiest I have ever seen her," William said beaming. "I can hardly wait."

"And your two are well?" Claveston asked James.

"George is a delightful devil and Emily, well she is so beautiful that I will probably always give her everything that she ever demands from me," the scarred former captain said with a delighted grin.

Claveston could hardly believe how much had changed, in such a short space of time. Not long ago, he and his friends had all been far from looking for wives, and hadn't even considered having children, yet now these were the things that made the two men before him content. He prayed he would be as blessed.

Miss Lefebvre and Lady Charlotte returned to the library only briefly, before everyone retired for the night. As he made to go upstairs, Claveston noticed that there was a light coming from under the door of his father's study. He went in, intending to extinguish it, to find his father seated at his desk, a large ledger in front of him. "You should go to bed, Papa," he told the duke.

"I just wanted to check this first," the older man said with a shrug. "It won't take me long."

Claveston turned to leave, then decided that this might be the perfect time to ask his father's permission to wed Miss Lefebvre. He took a deep breath and turned back. "Papa, I wish to ask Baron Lefebvre for his daughter's hand. I would like to ask your blessing to do so."

His father looked up from the ledger and grinned. "Well, I can't say I'm surprised," he said, standing up and moving around his desk. He slapped his son affectionately on the arm. "I rather guessed she was something special when you first demanded she and only she was suitable to be your sister's companion."

"Yet you still put her through the pain of thinking her a thief?" Claveston asked, not sure if he should be angry again, or just confused.

"I wish that had not ever happened, my boy," the duke said sadly. "Yet in some ways I am glad it did. It made you stand up and be the man I have always hoped you might become."

Claveston shook his head. He feared he would never understand his father. But he realized that he did not need to, as long as he could be wed to Sophie. "So, I have your blessing?"

"You do. And your mother's. She is fond of Miss Lefebvre. It is why she was so disappointed when it seemed that Miss Lefebvre was not the person that she had believed her to be. It broke her heart to think that one of the few people she has ever liked and allowed herself to trust could do such a thing. Your Mama does not make friends easily, you know that."

"I did not, I think I've always thought that her foreign friends and family were more important to her than we were," Claveston revealed unguardedly.

His father chuckled at his son's misunderstanding. "Quite the opposite, my boy. She travels so much, partly because she fears that others might get bored of her – and her greatest fear is that you and Gertrude might come to despise her if you spend too much time with her. She is a very complicated and insecure woman, your mother."

Strangely, his explanation made sense to Claveston. He had been surprised by Mama's reaction to the finding of the tiara. He had thought she knew Sophie better, that she would stand up for her. Yet that sense of betrayal must have been a heavy burden to bear. He had not always been too kind to his mother since, and he vowed to change that. Perhaps she was as much in need of knowing she was loved as he and Gertrude were.

CHAPTER SEVENTEEN

A letter from France had finally arrived. Claveston could hardly contain his delight when he read its contents. The past weeks had been amongst the hardest he'd ever had to bear, waiting for the permission he had longed for so greatly. He bounded up the stairs of the townhouse to his sister's room, where she and Miss Lefebvre were getting Gertrude ready for her visit to the Palace, to be presented at Court.

Gertrude had grown progressively more nervous as the date of her visit to St. James' drew closer, despite the successes she had achieved since her arrival in London for the Season. Mama had managed to get the essential vouchers for the entire family to be able to attend Almack's. Papa had somehow managed to always find a reason not to attend the meeting rooms, but Claveston had braved it in order to spend as much time as he could with Miss Lefebvre.

His presence had also given Gertrude confidence. He

had introduced her to everyone she needed to know in town, and she had settled into a small group of highly respectable young ladies who were all there for their first Season. The four had become fast friends, taking promenades in the park together and attending the same events wherever they could. Gertrude had been delighted to find out that all of her friends would be presented at Court on the same day as her. She was both nervous and excited about meeting Queen Charlotte, despite the ridiculousness of the rules that went with the event.

Claveston couldn't help himself from giggling when he saw the vast hoop and train of his sister's gown. The embroidery on the vast swathes of fabric was elaborate and beautifully done, but it was such an old-fashioned style, and it swamped his delicate sister. "Don't laugh," she scolded him. "I have no choice. Queen Charlotte insists upon the rules."

"You look like an elaborate sugar paste creation," Claveston teased. "But at least your gown for your party tonight suits you better. I am sure that young Harveston will be delighted to see you in it."

Gertrude blushed. Lord Alex Harveston was barely twenty and was heir to the Marquess of Bath. He was quite the most eligible bachelor in London this Season, and though very young seemed to be serious and sensible in a way most men his age were not. He had shown a particular interest in Gertrude, who tried to pretend that she thought little of the lad. But Miss Lefebvre had told Claveston that Gertrude was most certainly enamored with the boy. It would be an excellent match for her, though Claveston felt she was too young to be thinking of marriage.

"I shall go and check on Mama, the carriage will be here shortly. You will need to hurry," he warned them.

He left the room and headed to his Mama's suite of rooms. Mama was dressed ready to go and was spritzing herself with perfume at her dressing table as he arrived. "Mama, you look lovely," he said, kissing her cheek and looking at both their reflections in the mirror.

"Your father has promised me he will be back this evening for Gertrude's party," Mama said, glancing one last time in the mirror before she stood up and turned to look at him. "You will be there, too, will you not?"

"Of course," Claveston said handing her the letter he had just received. His mother smiled as she read it.

"Well, that is rather wonderful news, is it not?" she said, almost as delighted as he was himself.

"I thought I might ask her tonight, at Gertrude's party," he said cautiously. "Do you think that would be alright? I do not wish to overshadow Gertrude's day, but I do not think I can wait any longer before making Sophie my fiancée."

"I think she is adult enough now to see the good, don't you? I think your sister will be delighted to know that she is to gain a sister. It will be the perfect end to her big day." She tapped her finger to his cheek. Claveston beamed and bent his head to accept his mother's kiss. "Now, fetch your sister so we can get going. We must not be late."

Mama, Claveston, Sophie, and Gertrude bundled

into the carriage, which took them across London to St. James' Palace. A queue of young women and their families huddled in the courtyard, waiting to be called inside. Sophie and Claveston would have to watch the proceedings from a balcony, while Mama and Gertrude entered the Queens receiving room.

After kissing Gertrude and wishing her luck, the pair made their way up the stairway, as directed by a liveried footman. They took their seats. Sophie peered anxiously over the balcony. "There are so many young girls," she said, as she looked at the long line of them awaiting their turn. "What if the Queen does not 'ave enough time to greet them all?"

Claveston smiled. "She will. The greeting is brief. Each girl is announced and called forward. They and their sponsor curtsey, and the sponsor introduces the girl to the queen. Then the girl leaves the receiving room."

"All this expense, with the gowns and the hair, and the time and energy, for a two-minute greeting?" Sophie marveled. "I am glad I am French and did not 'ave to go through such a thing."

Claveston spied Gertrude and pointed her out to Sophie. His sister looked the demure young lady that Sophie had made of her, and Claveston couldn't have been more proud. Surreptitiously, he took Sophie's hand and gave it a squeeze. "You did that," he said nodding towards where Gertrude was dropping into a deep, elegant curtsey in front of Queen Charlotte.

He turned and saw that Sophie had tears in her eyes. He pulled out his handkerchief and dabbed them for her.

She smiled gratefully at him. "I could so easily 'ave left and not ever seen this," she said.

"But you did not, and you are here to see her. This is as much your triumph as hers and Mama's."

When they had seen that Gertrude and Mama had left the room, they squeezed past the other onlookers and made their way back downstairs. Gertrude's eyes were bright. "Queen Charlotte said I looked lovely, and that she had heard of what a credit I was to my Mama," she gushed. "She knew who I was. Lord Harveston is her nephew, or something, and he has spoken of me, she said."

"Our Gertrude has made her mark upon the London Season, she is the talk of *the Ton* it would seem," Mama said proudly. "But may we please go home and get out of these heavy gowns. Queen Charlotte may enjoy the formalities, but they are devilish to wear."

"And I must get ready for my party tonight. Everyone is to come," Gertrude said happily. "I can hardly wait. I shall dance all night."

"With young Harveston?" Claveston teased.

"I shall perhaps save him the dances before and after supper," Gertrude said, wafting her fan in front of her face coquettishly. "But I must not be seen to favor any one young man more than another." Everyone laughed and Gertrude pouted, knowing she was being teased, but then joined them.

THERE WAS no more than ten minutes before the first guests would be arriving, and Gertrude was being difficult. At the very last minute she had decided that her carefully pinned and curled hair was not as carefully pinned and curled as it needed to be and had insisted that Sophie and her lady's maid put it right.

"If you could just make them tighter, it is the fashion to have really tight curls," Gertrude said anxiously as Sophie heated up the curling irons in the fire.

"You look perfect as you are, the Queen thought as much," Sophie said, trying to placate Gertrude, who was fussing unnecessarily, in her mind.

"Sophie, please," Gertrude begged.

Sophie unpinned Gertrude's hair and picked up the silver hairbrush on the dresser and began to drag it through Gertrude's hair, undoing all the hard work that had been done earlier that day. She then began to re-pin it, following Gertrude's exacting directions as she demanded plaits and twists, flowers and seed pearls to be added in specific spots to catch the light.

A knock on the door made them all jump. Claveston peeked around the door. "Might I speak for a moment with Miss Lefebvre," he said, looking at Sophie who had a mouth full of hairpins and had not even changed from her day dress and apron. She nodded, glad of a moment's reprieve, and handed the curling irons to Gertrude's lady's maid and followed Claveston out into the hallway, removing the pins from her mouth as they went.

She smiled up at him, and as soon as she had pulled the door to, he stole a kiss. Sophie felt her skin flush with heat. He had not kissed her since her birthday, and they had barely seen one another since arriving in London. To be with him today, at the palace, holding his hand, had been the first inkling she had that he still felt the same way as he had declared that night. She had feared he had not meant it. That he had regretted it.

"I've had word from your father," he said, beaming.

"You wrote to him?" Sophie said, a little surprised that he should have done such a thing.

"I asked your permission to do so," he reminded her.

"I know, but I did not think you would actually do it. That you meant it. You've said nothing since. I presumed you 'ad just said it in the moment and that you did not really mean it."

"You either do not have a high opinion of me or assume that I do not have a high opinion of you." Claveston gave her an indulgent smile.

"It is not that," Sophie protested, but how could she possibly explain that it made no sense to her that a man such as him should care for her as she cared for him? "I..." she broke off, knowing she couldn't make sense of it herself, much less for him.

"I think so highly of you, my darling Sophie, that I asked my father for his permission that very night," he assured her. "And wrote to your father the next day. His reply took longer than I hoped – but that is for a very good reason. He waited to reply until he could arrange passage to England. He and your mother are coming to London, to see us wed – if you will agree to be my wife, that is."

He looked at her, beseeching her with his eyes. She

beamed. "My parents are coming here, to London? Oh, Lord Wycliffe, that is wonderful."

"I think you are forgetting something," he reminded her,

"I am?" she asked.

"There was something else I said in there, did you miss it?"

Sophie grinned but did not accept right away as he so obviously hoped she would. "Well, in order to agree," she said teasing him, "you will need to actually ask me if I wish to be married to you?" she said. He had not actually asked her outright and she was not going to answer a vague statement and assume anything.

He grinned, obviously seeing her point. He got down on one knee and took her hand. "Dear Miss Lefebvre, darling Sophie, will you be my wife? Will you love me, despite all my flaws? Please, say you will be mine? I have loved you for so long. I think I may have even fallen in love with you the night of William's wedding when you danced with me so beautifully. I have sought out reason after reason to keep you close to me ever since."

Sophie pulled him upright. "Dearest Claveston. 'ad you asked me when we first met, or even when I first came to Compton, I would 'ave turned you down. I did not much like you. You were often rude, always arrogant, and dressed entirely too flamboyantly – even for a Frenchwoman to bear." She laughed.

"Though your laugh is music to my ears, you are not giving me much confidence, Sophie," Claveston said, pretending to be pained by the somewhat hurtful things she had just said. He knew it was just her French tendency to be truthful, something he loved her for utterly.

"But, as I grew to know you," Sophie continued, pressing a finger to his lips so he would be quiet and let her speak, "I 'ave learned that you are kind and generous. You love your sister and do all you can to protect her, and always 'ave. You long only to be loved in return for the love you give – and I am 'appy to give you that love until the day that I die. I do love you, and I will marry you."

The door behind them clicked open as Claveston swept Sophie up into his arms and kissed her exuberantly all over her face. "Oh, I am so glad," Gertrude said behind them. "I couldn't stop myself from listening through the door, and I am so glad I did. I thought I might have ruined everything for you both, forever. I am so sorry I was such a shrew."

Claveston set Sophie down and hugged his sister as Sophie caught her breath. "You do know that you will never lose either of us now, don't you," he said to her.

"I do. I don't lose a brother, I gain a Sophie – forever," Gertrude said happily as Sophie embraced her, too. "But I will leave you alone now, I'm sorry for interrupting."

She disappeared back inside, and Claveston smiled at Sophie. "You will have to stop calling me Lord Wycliffe now," he reminded her as he took both her hands in his.

"I think I can manage that," she said a little shyly, "Claveston."

"I do so love the way my name sounds upon your lips," he sighed and stole another kiss from her perfect lips. "May I arrange for the banns to be read as soon as possible? I want to be able to marry you the moment your family arrives."

She nodded happily and watched him go downstairs ready to greet their guests. Sophie hugged herself and went back in to finish helping her new sister-in-law-to-be to get ready for her party. It would not be long before she would be enjoying her own big day, and with her family in attendance, too.

The day of the wedding dawned with heavy fog. But Sophie did not care. For her, the sun was shining as brightly as it ever had. She had been walking on air for weeks, ever since Claveston had proposed to her. She was in love and she was loved. Her parents had arrived just three days ago, laden down with gifts, eager to embrace and kiss Sophie over and over again.

Claveston had charmed them from the start, and they were so delighted about the upcoming wedding. Papa was pleased as punch to be able to give her away, at last, and Maman could hardly stop crying tears of happiness every time Sophie walked into a room. They were all staying in the London townhouse of the Duke of Mormont. Lady Charlotte and her father had made a joyful reacquaintance, and she had proudly introduced her son and daughter. Maman took to them straight away and George and Emily to her, the three were rarely to be parted.

Captain James and Lord William had accompanied

Charlotte, though Lady Mary had remained at Caldor, as her time was nigh, and they feared the travel would do her no good. Mr. and Mrs. Watts had sent gifts and much love, and Miss Knorr would be joining them on the day as she was already in London, acting as a companion for another young lady, now.

Sophie had rarely felt so surrounded by people she loved, and as she bathed in the tub, she marveled at how happy she was. It had been such a difficult time, and such a wonderful one, this past year. Much had happened, and much had been learned. She had feared that she would never find love yet had found it with a man she had believed would never know what it truly meant. And she knew he did love her, as she loved him.

She could so easily have lost everything. Without Claveston's love, without his faith in her, she could have been put out of Compton Hall – perhaps even found herself in front of a magistrate for a crime she had not committed, yet here she was now, marrying him, loving him, and a true member of his family in every way.

Gertrude burst into her bedchamber. "Good morning, sister," she chirruped as she held up a bath sheet so Sophie might get out of the tub. "Are you ready to be wed?"

"I am," Sophie admitted as she got out of the tub and pulled the bath sheet around her slender curves. "I can hardly believe it is 'appening, but I am ready for it."

"I know you have told me to stop apologizing to you, Sophie," Gertrude said, her face falling for a moment, her expression contrite. "But I really am sorry. I could have ruined everything for you and Claveston, and then you would both have been unhappy – or worse." She shuddered at the thought of how badly things might have gone. "I wish I had never done it, and I can assure you that I will never, ever do anything so foolish again."

"I know, Gertrude. You are a different girl to the one who did that," Sophie said warmly, swapping her sheet for a robe. She sat down at her dressing table and began to comb her wet hair through. "You 'ave grown up."

"I have," Gertrude said proudly. "I think Lord Alex may ask for my hand before the Season is done. Should I say yes?"

Sophie laughed. "How do you feel about marrying Lord Alex?" she asked.

"I like him. He is an excellent dancer, but..." she tailed off.

"But, what?"

"I don't think I am ready to be married," Gertrude said honestly. "I am still barely sixteen. This is only my first Season. I don't doubt that I like him, but if he really likes me, will we not still feel the same way next year?"

Sophie turned and caressed the girl's cheek. "Yes, you really 'ave grown up," she said. "I think that waiting is a very sensible thing to do."

Gertrude beamed. "I shall send in my maid to help you do your hair if you'd like me to?"

"That would be lovely. I should love to 'ave some of those tiny pearls in my hair to match my gown," she admitted.

"Oh, that would look lovely," Gertrude agreed and bounced off again, as Maman appeared in the doorway.

"You look lovely, my darling," she said tenderly, kissing Sophie's cheeks and caressing them gently.

"I've not done anything more than 'ave a bath," Sophie said grinning.

"A woman in love 'as a glow, do you not think?" Maman said.

"Per'aps," Sophie agreed. "I am so glad that you and Papa are here."

"We would not 'ave missed this day for anything," Maman said. "You are our little girl, and we are delighted you 'ave found a good man who loves you and will take care of you."

The next few hours passed in the twinkle of an eye, as people hurried in and out of Sophie's rooms, doing her hair, helping her into her dress, spraying her with scent, and chattering about all manner of things. Charlotte was the last person to come in, as everyone else disappeared to get ready themselves and to depart for the church. "You truly do look radiant," Charlotte said. "I am almost glad I let you go so you could find such happiness."

"Almost?" Sophie queried.

"I have missed you terribly. Can you not convince Claveston to buy a property near us in Alnerton so I might see you more often?"

Sophie smiled. "I can try," she said. "I must confess, it would be the very best wedding gift I could ask of him."

"Are you ready?"

"I am."

Sophie stood and the two friends walked down the stairs together, arm in arm. Papa was waiting for her in the hallway, with tears in his eyes. He hugged her tightly and in a choked voice told her how much he loved her. "I love you, too, Papa," Sophie said, trying hard not to cry along with him. "But don't fret. I am so happy, and now I shall be able to come and see you more often as Claveston and his family often travel all over the world. I am sure I can convince him to take me to France from time to time."

"I should like that," Papa said happily.

The three of them got into the open landau waiting for them outside. Passersby hollered greetings and good luck as they passed by, making Sophie feel very special. As they reached the church, she could see the faces of everyone she loved most in the world, and the tears began to pour down her cheeks. Papa wiped them for her, and Charlotte reapplied the light touch of rouge that he had accidentally wiped away with her tears, and they got out of the carriage.

All of a sudden, Sophie felt nervous. Her stomach churned and she began to shake. Papa clasped her hand on his arm tightly and gave her a reassuring wink. She smiled at him and they went into the church. Immediately she saw Claveston at the altar, her nerves disappeared. She looked into his eyes and saw only love. And she knew that was what she would always see every time she looked at him.

When Papa placed her hand in Claveston's, Sophie felt whole. "I love you," she whispered to him as the minister began to cry out the opening prayers.

"I love you," he whispered back. "You are perfect."

The ceremony seemed to pass in the wink of an eye. All too soon they were walking down the aisle of the church and out into bright sunshine. Sophie turned her face up to it, enjoying the warmth on her skin. "I bought you a gift," Claveston said as he pulled out a rolled document from inside his jacket. He handed it to her.

Sophie removed the wax seal carefully and unrolled it. She read it slowly, then turned to beam at her husband. "You bought us an 'ouse in Alnerton," she said, utterly delighted. "Charlotte and I were just joking about such a thing before the ceremony."

"I know how much you love it there, and the people. We will have to spend much of our time here in London, and at Compton, but I see no reason why we can't spend some there, too."

"You know me so well," she said reaching up on tiptoes and kissing him warmly.

"I have learned to listen," he said kissing her back and sweeping her up into his arms. He lifted her into the carriage and set her down upon the bench. "I love you, Lady Sophie, with all my heart."

"And I love you with all of mine," she echoed, unable to stop smiling as he got into the carriage beside her and put his arms around her. Wherever she was now, as long as she was with him, she would be at home and he would never need to wish for love ever again, as she would give it to him freely every day of their lives.

SOPHIE GOT her happy ever after although it didn't seem like that would happen! Did you miss the first book in this series? Please check out Loving the Scarred Soldier

MY DEAR READER

Thank you for reading and supporting my books! I hope this story brought you some escape from the real world into the always captivating Regency world. A good story, especially one with a happy ending, just brightens your day and makes you feel good! If you enjoyed the book, would you leave a review on Amazon? Reviews are always appreciated.

Below is a complete list of all my books! Why not click and see if one of them can keep you entertained for a few hours?

The Duke's Daughters Series
The Duke's Daughters: A Sweet Regency Romance
Boxset
A Rogue for a Lady
My Restless Earl
Rescued by an Earl
In the Arms of an Earl
The Reluctant Marquess (Prequel)

A Smithfield Market Regency Romance
The Smithfield Market Romances: A Sweet Regency
Romance Boxset
The Rogue's Flower

Saved by the Scoundrel
Mending the Duke
The Baron's Malady

The Returned Lords of Grosvenor Square
The Returned Lords of Grosvenor Square: A Regency
Romance Boxset
The Waiting Bride
The Long Return
The Duke's Saving Grace
A New Home for the Duke

The Spinsters Guild
A New Beginning
The Disgraced Bride
A Gentleman's Revenge
A Foolish Wager
A Lord Undone

Convenient Arrangements
A Broken Betrothal
In Search of Love
Wed in Disgrace
Betrayal and Lies
A Past to Forget
Engaged to a Friend

Landon House
Mistaken for a Rake
A Selfish Heart
A Love Unbroken

A Christmas Match
A Most Suitable Bride
An Expectation of Love

Second Chance Regency Romance
Loving the Scarred Soldier
Second Chance for Love
A Family of her Own

Christmas Stories
Love and Christmas Wishes: Three Regency Romance
Novellas
A Family for Christmas
Mistletoe Magic: A Regency Romance
Home for Christmas Series Page

Happy Reading!
All my love,
Rose

A SNEAK PEAK OF LOVING
THE SCARRED SOLDIER

C aldor House, Alnerton, 1807

"I WILL GET YOU, Lady Charlotte Pierce," James whispered into her ear as he leaned just a smidge closer.

Charlotte looked over her shoulder to where Mrs. Crosby, her plump companion, was walking some feet behind them.

"Oh no you will not, James Watts, for I already have you," Charlotte replied cheekily, a playful grin on her face which exaggerated her dimples and the small cleft in her chin.

"Ah, but you only think that you have me. Truth be told, I have already laid claim to you these many years, but I allowed you to believe otherwise." He raised his chin slightly, the sun shining down on his handsome face. "There is no escaping it."

James folded his arms behind his back and Charlotte

peered up at him. James and her brother William were the same age, but James was minutely taller, with broader shoulders and a more relaxed air about him. William, unfortunately, was often far too austere – a characteristic for which he could thank their father, the Duke of Mormont.

Charlotte kept watching James in silence, waiting until he turned back in her direction. The moment he did, she grinned at him and promptly stuck out her tongue.

"You always like to best me James, but I tell you, one day, I will be the one who claims victory. Not you."

He grinned, his bright smile illuminating his oval face and gently sloping cheekbones.

"I look forward to it. You could win me over for the rest of my life," he whispered.

Charlotte's heart fluttered in her chest.

"You should not say such things, James," she replied. "Someone might think you mean what you say."

Her fingers rose to coil a tress of dark brown hair. She wrapped it around her index finger several times as she kept her eyes to the ground, waiting for his reply.

"You know I always mean what I say," he answered tersely.

Charlotte's feet faltered with her heart. What was he saying? Lately, James's conversations were more and more personal, much more than they ever had been before. They'd long had a closeness between them, ever since her former governess, Mrs. Northam, had married his father, John, who acted as the Duchy of Mormont's solicitor. Now, however, things were changing.

Slowly, she looked up at him again and was met by the intensity of his emerald eyes. It made her heart gallop. She could not maintain the connection and quickly looked away.

"James, do not toy with me."

"I would never toy with you about such things," he replied calmly.

Again, Charlotte's eyes could not refrain from looking at him. In recent years she had often found herself admiring the man he had become. He was no longer the boy she'd run after and played games with all those years ago. He was a man of twenty, two years her elder, and more esteemed in her sight than any of their acquaintances, save her brother.

Charlotte stopped walking when she realized that James had failed to follow. She turned to face him, perplexity filling her heart. These feelings were strange to her. She had no mother to teach her, and with Mrs. Northam, now Mrs. Watts, no longer in her family employ, she was left to decipher the world on her own, for her nurse, Mrs. Crosby, was not someone whom she felt she could ask about important matters.

"Charlotte."

The sound of her name on his lips was a cherished utterance. She was very fond of it, more than she ever dared to admit. They knew each other too well - what she felt could not be what she thought it was. Could it? When he looked at her the way he was doing now, she believed that it could be.

"We have known each other for what seems a lifetime," James continued. The soft timbre of his voice was soothing. "We have played together and argued, cried, and laughed. We have seen each other in every... circumstance."

She laughed as the memory of their foray into his family's lakes, in nothing more than their undergarments as children suddenly flashed into her mind. Her father had been most upset by the indiscreet incident, which had left her soaked through, on the eve of a special dinner party. He had been equally displeased with the subsequent chill that had confined her to her bed. None of which had bothered her.

"We have."

James' brow furrowed slightly and she had the urge to smooth the wrinkles with her thumb. Customarily, she would have done so, but at that moment, with her feelings teetering on the brink, she dared not, lest they both fall over the edge.

Charlotte watched in curious fascination as the lump in James' throat bobbed up and down, and her dashing friend, ever confident, seemed to falter in his words. It was surprisingly endearing to see him so undone. She bit back a smile, but still felt the tug of it on her cheeks.

"You have to know... that is... you must be aware," James stuttered. His eyes were still lowered to his feet, but then, in a sudden burst of confidence, he forced himself to meet her gaze.

"Aware of what?" Charlotte questioned.

It took all of her strength to muster the words of the questions which curiosity demanded be answered. Did he feel as she did? Did his heart flutter at the sight of her as hers did whenever she saw him? Did he get cold, and his skin prickle when they touched? Was his head as full of her as hers was of him?

The more she thought of it, the more her emotions threatened to get the better of her. She quickly turned away, sure that her feelings were now evident on her face. She did not want to lose to him in this. She did not want to be the first to make her feelings known. In this one thing, she wanted to best him.

Charlotte's heart thundered in her ears. Her hands folded into defiant fists, as she determined not to be swayed by her emotions. She would be strong. She would let him speak and not give herself away, though she was aware that she may have already done so.

"Charlotte?" James' voice was a whisper. Then, she felt his hands settle gently on her arms. She was acutely aware of the proximity of his body to hers. This was not their normal interaction. Yes, they were close, had even embraced, but the feelings which filled her at that moment were far greater, more powerful – consuming. Her stomach felt as if it would take flight. "You feel it too, don't you?" he continued to whisper.

"Feel what?" Charlotte replied as her voice shook.

She glanced in the direction of Mrs. Crosby. The woman was pretending to look at the leaves on one of the potted plants, but glances in their direction made Charlotte aware that she was keeping a close eye on them, in case things went too far.

"She will not come. I asked her not to."

Charlotte's eyes widened and her breath caught in her throat at James' confession.

"You did what?"

"I asked Mrs. Crosby to give us a moment of privacy," he continued. "There is something very particular which I wish to say to you, Charlotte. Something best said to your face and not your back."

She could hear the slight lilt of laughter in his voice, but also nervousness.

"James," she replied. "You can tell me anything. You always have."

Her words were answered with a gentle tug on her arms, turning her to face him. She did not resist. She could not. All strength was gone from her limbs and she was at the mercy of her feelings, which would not be hidden.

Their eyes met and Charlotte thought she might faint. Her head felt light, her heart was gone, only large butterfly wings remained, beating frantically in her chest, as smaller ones filled her belly. What was happening?

He did not remove his hands from her arms, Instead, he stepped closer, and Charlotte felt sure that the world had stopped and she no longer remembered how to breathe.

"You and William have always been my dearest friends," James stated. "But you, Charlotte, you have become something infinitely more dear to me." Warmth washed up her neck and she was sure that her cheeks were now painted in crimson. Yet she could not speak. "I know that you have only ever considered me as a friend, and for a long time, I had accepted that fact. I thought I could live with it, but I cannot. I cannot be content with simply being your friend when I desire to be something much more."

Charlotte raised a hand and placed it on his chest to stop him, but the beating beneath her fingers caused her to pause. His heart was racing just like hers.

James looked at her delicate fingers and then placed his hand over hers, holding it over his heart.

"This is what I feel every time I am near you. I cannot stop it. I have tried, but nothing works. I think it is because I do not wish it to. I like that you do this to me. You are the only one who can."

Her breathing erratic, Charlotte tried to think. She knew all the proper things to do, the decorum that was required, but how did one have such decorum with someone who had nursed your wounds and wiped your tears, often after having been responsible for causing them? One who knew you better than anyone else did?

"I know there are many who desire you," James continued. "I am not so foolish as to believe that I am the only one who cares for you, but I would hope I might have some advantage over those others."

"Of whom do you speak? I know of no one," Charlotte questioned, bewildered.

His emerald eyes were ablaze.

"Do you mean to tell me that there is no other who wishes your hand?"

Charlotte's hearing became hollow, only the sound of what seemed to be rushing water could be heard as the words left his lips. She was eighteen. She had never had anyone desire her hand, at least not that she knew of. Such matters were for her father, and none dared speak to her before presenting their proposal to him. None but James, that is. He was allowed certain liberties that other gentlemen were not, being such a close family friend.

"What are you saying?" she whispered, "Be plain."

He smiled at her.

"Always so straightforward."

"Always skirting around the subject," she replied. "Just tell me. Do not keep me on tenterhooks." She squeezed his hand lightly. "I want to hear the words."

James stepped closer, the space between them almost entirely gone as he lowered his head to her ear and whispered.

"I love you, Charlotte. I have always loved you."

The smile his words elicited could not be contained, and as their eyes met, she answered him.

"I love you, too, James. I always have."

~

CALDOR HOUSE, *Alnerton, 1809*

"LADY CHARLOTTE. LADY CHARLOTTE." A soft voice repeated her name, but Charlotte was doing her utmost to resist. "You must rouse yourself, Lady Charlotte. The day is already upon us and you must get ready."

It was Sophie Lefebvre, her new companion. Her father had finally been swayed to Charlotte's view that Mrs. Crosby was no longer suitable and that a woman closer to her age would be a far better choice. Sophie, who was also almost twenty, the daughter of an English-woman and a Frenchman, her family in exile from

France as a result of the war, had seemed a good choice to replace Mrs. Crosby.

Charlotte forced her dark brown eyes open. The room was still mostly in darkness, but Sophie had the chambermaids already at work opening the blinds, while she set about laying out Charlotte's attire in readiness.

"Please, Lady Charlotte. You do not want to keep your brother and the duke waiting. It would be disrespectful to Monsieur Watts if you were to arrive late," Sophie pleaded. "You would not want to do that."

Sophie knew those words would force Charlotte from her bed, though no words could change how Charlotte felt, not on that day.

Charlotte forced herself to rise from her four-poster bed, then padded to the window, her bare feet making no noise as she crossed the room. She looked out to where grey mists covered the gardens. The sky was overcast and the sun was completely hidden. It was as if the day shared her feelings.

"Quickly, Lady Charlotte," Sophie continued. She came to stand beside Charlotte. "I know that you do not wish to go, but you must."

"Must I?" Charlotte retorted weakly. "It will change nothing."

Sophie sighed.

"No, it will not. It is not supposed to. It is for you to show the respect which Monsieur Watts deserves. Please, come from the window and let me help you dress."

Charlotte was a doll in Sophie's hands. She turned her and twisted her, made her sit, and stand, all while Charlotte uttered not a word. Finally, once her shoes were on and her black dress laced and every adornment in place, she sat her before the mirror.

The young woman who looked back at her was foreign to her eyes. Her skin was far paler than it used to be. Her eyes less bright and her long dark brown hair seemed a dull greyish-black. Everything seemed to be cast in shades of grey.

The white collar which rose around her neck itched, but Charlotte cared little about it. It was the only contrast to the black of the rest of her ensemble. Once her hair was curled and pinned, Sophie placed a black feathered cap on her head.

"C'est fini! You are done!"

Charlotte didn't reply. Instead, she stood and strode out of her chamber.

She found William loitering in the hall, waiting for her. Her brother was not himself either, as was evident from the solemn expression on his face. He walked toward her and took her hand, hooking it gently over his arm.

"How are you this morning, Charlotte? We missed you at breakfast."

"How should I be?" she answered absently.

Her eyes glanced over the balcony to the floor below.

"It was a foolish question," William replied. "Forgive me. I do not know how to deal with these matters."

She turned to her brother.

"Save Mother, we are unaccustomed to such things. You are forgiven."

He smiled at her before proceeding, in silence, to escort her down the stairs and out the door, to where the carriage waited for them. It was decorated appropriately; pulled by matched black horses with black plumes upon their heads. The driver was similarly dressed in black and the carriage was of the same color.

Charlotte's feet faltered, but William bore her up and helped her inside. Their father was already waiting.

"That took you too long," he commented harshly. "It isn't right to be late for such things. It is gross disrespect, Charlotte. You should know better. Both of you."

"Forgive me, Father," William replied. "It was my fault entirely."

"All the worse. You, being the elder, should direct your sister appropriately, and not pander to such poor conduct. See to it that it never happens again."

"Of course, Father. Never again," William replied.

Charlotte remained silent, and as the carriage moved forward, her gaze stayed fixed out the window.

She recognized none of the landscape as they passed, her mind too full to allow her to truly see what was before her, and she shunned the sight of Watton Hall, James' former home. She could not look upon it without losing her composure. She chose to close her eyes until she was sure they were well past it. The next sight she saw, consequently, was that of Alnerton Village Church.

The chapel was overflowing with mourners, but a special place had been reserved for them, and William helped her to it. Charlotte sat in silence, refusing to look at the empty coffin at the front of the church.

James was not there. His body had been lost somewhere in Roliça, Portugal, where he'd fallen during the battle with the French the year before. It had taken months for them to get news of his death, and more still for his father to come to terms with it, enough to have the memorial service held.

They all struggled to believe it – Captain James Watts, a fine young man, his father's pride and joy, an adoring stepson and caring and devoted friend, and the man Charlotte loved, was dead.

The Reverend Moore said a great many things about James, but they were only shadows of the truth. James was far more than the vicar claimed. The vicar hadn't known James as she did.

She could have told them of the man he truly was, the gentle soul who'd tended her knee when she fell among the brambles. The man who'd taken every opportunity to touch her hand whenever he could, and who had loved to make her laugh.

The man whose face she still saw every time she closed her eyes.

Once the rites were performed, Charlotte and her family gathered with Mr and Mrs Watts to bury the son they'd lost.

She was coping, in control, until the moment the pall-bearers brought the coffin to the grave. Then, Charlotte lost all semblance of calm.

The tears flowed from her eyes and her body was wracked with uncontrollable spasms. She gasped for breath but found none. She was suffocating where she stood. The air she struggled to breathe was gone. James was gone.

William did his best to console her, but there was no consolation for her grief - it was a physical pain she could not bear, and she crumbled under the weight of it. Seconds later, her brother's strong arms were carrying her away from the sight, away from sympathetic, pitying eyes, to the safety of their carriage. Their father followed close behind, and soon they were on their way home.

Charlotte had no recollection of the return journey. Her room was dark when she awoke, much later, and she was still dressed in her mourning gown. Her feathered cap was gone.

She rolled onto her back but no sooner had she done so than fresh tears rolled down her cheeks. He was gone. James was never coming back.

It was heartbreak like no other. She had been a child, barely two, when her mother had passed away, and she had no true recollection of that loss. James, though, was different. She had known him. She had cared for him. She had loved him.

Silent tears kept her company as she lay in the dark until her eyes could weep no more. Then, Charlotte forced herself to sit up. The gloom of her room was oppressive - she needed to escape it, she needed light to help her fight the darkness which threatened to overtake her. She rushed to her chamber door, forgetting to don stockings or shoes, and simply walked along the corridor with no plan of where she was going.

Soon, she heard her father's voice. She followed it until she stood outside his office. She listened; he was in conversation with someone - her brother William she was sure - and she heard her name mentioned.

"The Marquess of Dornthorpe?" her brother asked.

"Yes. He has written to propose his interest in an

alliance between our families. He is seeking your sister's hand for his son, Malcolm, Earl of Benton."

"Father, it is too soon to present such a proposal to Charlotte. She is still mourning for James."

"She will recover. Such an alliance should be most agreeable to all parties. However, I note your point. I will give her a few weeks to mourn his loss before informing her of the betrothal."

"Betrothal? Father, don't you think it prudent to ask Charlotte if she has any interest in the man before arranging an engagement. She has met him but four times, if I remember right. And a betrothal during mourning – that will set the gossips' tongues wagging."

"Four times was more than enough for your mother to decide to marry me. I do not see why your sister should be any different. As for the gossips – well, technically, James is no relation of ours, and so mourning is not a requirement."

"Father, please..."

"I have made my decision, William. Your sister will marry Malcolm Tate, and become the Countess of Benton, and eventually the Marchioness of Dornthorpe. Our family will sit on two seats, Dornthorpe and Mormont. Such a fortunate alliance is to be envied indeed."

Her knees gave out and the floor rushed up, as Charlotte slumped against the wall. That was it? James was barely in his grave and yet she was given to another? It was at that moment that she realized how conniving her father truly was. He cared nothing for her pain and hurt, only for their family's good standing.

Charlotte had no strength to remove herself from outside the door. *Let them find me here,* she thought. *Let them know that I am aware of what they had discussed without her. Let them see what it has done to me. Maybe that would touch father's heart.*

She might hope so, but she suspected it was unlikely.

CHAPTER ONE

C aldor House, Alnerton, 1814

CHARLOTTE LOOKED up at the imposing building toward which they were driving. Caldor House was still the same, all these years later, and as it had in the past, it filled her heart with heaviness. The only reason she was returning to her father's home was for the sake of her son. George needed a male influence, and without his father, he had only her father and William to guide him, for her late husband's father now had suffered a debilitating illness.

She looked over to where her sleeping child lay. He was so much like Malcolm that it made her smile to think of it. She stroked his hair gently. She had not loved Malcolm when she'd married him, but he was the escape she'd needed – from grief and from loneliness.

In return, she had given him the gift of their son – the

son he had hoped for, to carry on his family name. She was happy that she'd been able to do so before his time on earth was over. Her only regret was that he would not be there to see George grow into a man he would be proud of.

The carriage stopped on the broad expanse of gravel in front of the house. The door opened, and there, standing in his usual fine attire, was her brother William. A broad smile spread across his face as he immediately took the stairs at a rapid pace to come toward her.

"Charlotte!" he called.

She smiled in return as the coachman opened the door for her and helped her down.

"William, how wonderful to see you."

She wrapped her arms around him. It felt like a lifetime since they had last seen each other, and she had missed him dearly - it was his presence here, more than anything, which had brought her back to her childhood home.

"How was your journey?" William asked.

"Long and tiring. George is asleep in the carriage," Charlotte replied.

"Then I shall gather him up and carry him into the house."

William strode toward the carriage and, moments later, cradled her son in his arms. George looked angelic, nestled against his uncle's chest, completely safe from all harm.

It wasn't easy being alone and so far from home. Once Malcolm had died, everything had changed. Suddenly the security Charlotte knew no longer existed.

There was also the threat from those who wished to take from her son what was rightfully his, the title of Earl of Benton, and, likely quite soon, that of Marquess of Dornthorpe, when his ailing grandfather died. He was too young, but he would learn under her father, and when he was old enough, he would return and take his place. In the meantime, Malcolm's trusted steward, Mr. Charlesworth, was tending to matters and would send Charlotte regular reports.

"He weighs nothing," William commented as they walked up the stairs.

"To you perhaps, but to me, he weighs little less than a ton," Charlotte mused. "Is Father at home?"

William's expression fell.

"He had to remain in town to see to some pressing matters with our bankers. I have only just returned myself. I wanted to be here for your arrival. Father will return by tea time."

Charlotte nodded in understanding - it was for the best that her father was not present. It gave her time to settle herself, to some extent, before seeing him again. Since her marriage, Charlotte had seen little of her father. He had stayed in Alnerton or at their townhouse in London and found no reason to visit her, not even at the birth of his grandson, although he had sent a card and an expensive gift.

"I have prepared your old rooms for you and converted the adjoining suite into a nursery for George. I thought it best to keep him near you. He will be unfamiliar with these surroundings for a time."

Charlotte smiled.

"Thank you, William. You think of everything."

"I try to," he replied with a grin. "Especially when it comes to matters of my sister and nephew."

They were greeted at the door by almost all of the household staff, their smiling faces bright as they welcomed her back. Charlotte was slightly overwhelmed. She'd almost forgotten them, for she had put Caldor House behind her on the day she'd left, thinking she would never return to it. Unfortunately, fate had other plans for her, and here she was.

Once the welcome was over, she followed William upstairs as footmen scurried to unload all of her possessions and carry the steamer trunks up to her rooms. William carried George into the nursery and settled him into bed without him even waking. Leaving a nursemaid watching over him as he slept, William opened the door and ushered her through into her rooms.

The space was bright, the curtains pulled wide to allow the sun into the room, but the memories lingered there. She could remember the last night she'd spent in that room, and the many before that, filled with hopes, fears, and then abiding grief.

I thought never to see this room again, yet, here I am.

"Is everything to your liking?" William said from behind her.

Charlotte turned to him, slowly untying the ribbon from beneath her chin as she removed her bonnet.

"Everything is just as I remember it."

"I wanted it to be as easy an adjustment for you as possible."

He smiled at her.

"I missed you very much," Charlotte replied.

Sadness began to prick her eyes with tears.

"And I, you," William replied as she strode toward him.

She fell into her brother's embrace and held him tightly as memories overwhelmed her. His hand gently patted her back as he spoke soothingly in her ear.

"I know it has been frightfully difficult for you, Charlotte. I wish I could have made it better. A thousand times I have wished I could have changed the things that happened, but I hope you know I had no control over those circumstances."

"Hush," Charlotte urged. "Do not speak of it. I know what you would have done if you could." She looked up at him. "Now, leave me alone for a while. I shall rest before tea."

"Of course."

William nodded and excused himself.

She lay back on the bed intending to rest, but her mind resisted that intent. Memories tumbled through her mind, leaving her wide awake and out of sorts. She lay on her bed, her hands clasped over her stomach as she looked up at the canopy above her, until the exhaustion from the long day of travel, and all that had gone before, caught up with her, and sleep overtook her.

It was nearly teatime when Charlotte awoke. Immediately, she worried about George, but when she called for the maid, she was assured that George had eaten his meal, had looked in to see his mother sleeping, and had happily gone back into the nursery with the maid, to play with his toys.

Charlotte allowed the maid to dress her in a gown suitable for dining with her father. Her father kept an elegant table at all times and expected everyone to conform to his expectations.

Her dress was mint green in color, made from the finest silk and lace. It had been a gift from Malcolm before he became ill. Charlotte was glad that, now her mourning was done, she could wear colors again. The year of mourning had taken a toll on her, shut away at Bentonmere Park, but it had also been peaceful. Now, for George's sake, it was time to be visible to the world again.

She smoothed her hands over her stomach as she looked at her reflection in the mirror. Her shape had changed after having George. She no longer had a girl's figure, but it was a pleasing figure nonetheless. She twisted a curl of dark hair around her finger then pushed it back into place before turning away.

The dining room was set when Charlotte arrived. William lingered by the door waiting for her.

"Father isn't here as yet," he informed her.

"Shall we sit then and wait?"

"We may as well. You know how he is about punctuality, even if he is not so himself," her brother answered with a light laugh.

He hooked his arm and held it out to her.

Charlotte allowed her brother his little trifles of amusement. He'd had so little of humor in his youth, for he'd lived under their father's thumb, ever aware that he was to inherit his title and position, as Duke, and also his vast portfolio of investments, in banking and shipping. It had always been a heavy burden for William to bear, and because of that, Charlotte hardly ever allowed herself the luxury of sharing her burdens with her brother.

James had always been the person she'd shared such things with.

The thought of her former love gave her a moment of pause. It always did. Despite his death, James Watts had really never left her, even throughout her marriage, he was, in a way, ever-present. He was still a comfort to her in her thoughts, even if he was no longer in the world.

"How are Father's affairs?" she questioned once they were seated.

William sighed.

"When it comes to matters pertaining to the smooth running of the Duchy, it is never a straightforward task. Father insists upon seeing to every detail, no matter how small. He leaves me little responsibility – though he expects me to pay as close attention as he does himself."

She looked at him with concern. He was clearly frustrated at the lack of trust their father was showing him.

"Do you like it at all? Working with Father, I mean?"

"There are days when I love it. Learning about all the elements involved in the Duchy's management, from managing the rents to investing the proceeds from the land well – it is absorbing and challenging. Many in Father's place would entrust such work to managers and bailiffs – but he prides himself that it is a matter of honor."

"Has there been some cause for a loss?"

Charlotte shook her head lightly. Her brother was a clever man. He had left Cambridge with high praise from his tutors, and he was not one to shirk his duties. But

Father was very demanding. It could only be hard on William to have to always listen and never be permitted to give his opinion or have any autonomy.

They were sipping wine and talking when their father finally arrived. He marched into the room without care or apology and promptly seated himself at the head of the table.

"Charlotte," he stated. "I am glad to see that you that have arrived and remembered how I prefer to go on here."

"Thank you, Father."

"Where is the boy?"

"George is with Mrs. White, his nurse. He will be in bed by now."

"Good, a boy needs routine and order - structure makes a man," her father continued. He picked up the small bell which sat to his right and rang it, as an indication to the staff to serve dinner.

The meal was delicious - four courses as usual - including dessert. Her father always insisted upon it, although why she never knew. It was simply the way it was.

"How is Mrs. Watts, William? Has she improved at all?" her father asked through a mouthful of the roast.

"I'm afraid not, Father. Mr Watts told me only yesterday that she has taken a turn for the worse."

"Unfortunate. We are sure to have a funeral to attend soon," her father continued.

Charlotte dropped her knife in alarm.

"Funeral? Is Mrs. Watts so ill?"

"I am afraid so," William explained. "It has been

several months now since she first became ill and there seems to be no end in sight. I am sorry to have to tell you this on your first day back."

She could hardly think. Beatrice Watts was the only mother figure Charlotte had ever known. The thought of her death was unbearable. How would her husband take that news after already having lost James?

"I will go to see her tomorrow," Charlotte blurted.

It was her father's turn to drop his cutlery. However, he recovered quickly and carried on as if nothing had happened.

"I do not think that is wise, Charlotte. Mrs. Watts is very ill and you have a child to consider. You cannot allow yourself to be so exposed."

"What exposure can there be, Father? I will take the customary precautions. I am sure that you and William have visited her, and neither of you has become ill."

"I think Father is correct, Charlotte. You have only just returned here, perhaps you should allow yourself some time to adjust before visiting the Watts," William agreed.

She looked at him perplexed.

"William, Mrs. Watts has tended to us our entire lives. How can I be so unfair as to avoid her, especially under these circumstances? I cannot. I will not. I shall visit her tomorrow."

The subject died immediately, but Charlotte did not miss the silent exchange between her brother and father, an exchange of looks which puzzled her completely. She did not understand their thinking but she would not be persuaded by it. Mrs. Watts was a lovely woman and she would see her, and care for her if it would give her any comfort at all.

After tea, Charlotte retreated to the parlor, but she was not alone for long. Mrs. White brought George to her soon after, the young child having woken fretful and calling for her. She set her son on the floor with his blocks and joined him.

"A little of this and you will be tired again in no time, won't you George?" she said as she placed one block on top of the other. George hit the floor with his.

They continued like that for several minutes before they were joined by William. Her brother watched them with a silent grin as they played. His presence was comforting and Charlotte was happy to have him there and thankful that their father was absent.

"I am sorry I could not stay long after the funeral," William said suddenly.

Charlotte looked at him perplexed.

"Why do you bring it up?"

"I do not think I have apologized enough for it. You needed me after his passing and I could not be there for you as I should."

"William, you had pressing work. I understood," Charlotte assured him.

William had only stayed a fortnight after Malcolm was laid to rest. Charlotte had wanted him to stay longer, but the management of the estates and the investments had called him away, and she could not bring herself to ask him to prolong his stay regardless. She held no grudge toward him for it. It was the way of the world, and her loss was no large factor in his life, only hers.

"Thank you, Charlotte. You have always been too kind in everything," William continued. "Do you still intend to visit Mrs. Watts tomorrow?"

"Of course," she replied. "I said I would and I shall do so. I shall make arrangements in the morning to visit her during the afternoon."

William was silent for a moment. Charlotte could see he was contemplating something, more than likely the bank, or next year's crop plantings on one of the estates – he never stopped thinking of such things, it seemed to her.

"Will you excuse me, Charlotte? I have a matter I must urgently attend to."

"Of course."

William came to them and ruffled George's hair before leaving the room. Charlotte remained with her son, playing with his blocks until his eyes grew heavy again, and he curled beside her on the floor to sleep.

She lifted George and carried him from the room, leaving the blocks where they lay, holding his head gently against her shoulder as she walked toward the stairs and their rooms. On her way up, she happened to turn, and glance down, to see William giving a letter to a footman, who immediately left the house. Her brow furrowed. Who was William writing to at such an hour?

THERE IS a huge secret that Lady Charlotte discovers and it will change her life! Check out the rest of the story in the Kindle Store Loving the Scarred Soldier

Made in the USA
Middletown, DE
21 June 2021